MARCUS AND MIRIAM

MARCUS AND MIRIAM

A STORY OF JESUS

REBECCA RUTER SPRINGER

www.whitecrowbooks.com

Marcus and Miriam

First published in 1908 by David C. Cook Publishing Co.
This copyright © 2025 by White Crow Productions Ltd. All rights reserved.
Published by White Crow Books, an imprint of White Crow Productions Ltd.

The right of the author has been asserted in accordance with
the Copyright, Design and Patents act 1988.

No part of this book may be reproduced, copied or used in any form
or manner whatsoever without written permission, except in the
case of brief quotations in reviews and critical articles.

A CIP catalogue record for this book is available from the British Library.
For information, contact White Crow Books by e-mail: info@whitecrowbooks.com.

Cover Design by Astrid@Astridpaints.com
Interior design by Velin@Perseus-Design.com

Hardback: ISBN: 9781786772787
Paperback: ISBN: 9781786772794
eBook: ISBN: 9781786772800

Fiction / Christian

www.whitecrowbooks.com

To
Our Granddaughter,
Constance,
and to
All others who love
Our Lord Jesus Christ
This story is lovingly dedicated.

Also by the author:
Intra Muros (My Dream of Heaven).
Beechwood.
Self.
Songs by the Sea.

Introduction

by Rev. Henry R. Naylor, D. D.,

of Washington, D. C.

~

This is really a story of Jesus and his friends; an amplification and simplification of the account given by the Evangelists, beautiful in its simplicity and naturalness. The author has brought to her task a keen power of analysis and a wealth of illustrative material which brings out the real characters of the New Testament, causing them to occupy their right places in the reader's mind, and thus affording much suggestive help to the better understanding of the Scriptures. Here is seen not the "mere man" but the "real man"; and we see at once how he could be "touched with our infirmities." Here also may be found the answer to the oft-repeated question, "Why did the people love him?" The gentle, beneficent spirit of the man who spent his life doing good is so faithfully delineated that we are not surprised to find all the people, except his bitter enemies, following his steps and hanging upon his words.

The book will enrich the sacred literature of this and coming time, and will be read with pleasure and profit by both young and old, for in it are "apples of gold set in pictures of silver."

H. R. N.

Author's Preface

Among all Bible students, among all professed Christians, there is a feeling of deep regret that the human side of the life of Christ, as given by the Evangelists, is not more complete in detail, especially in regard to his private life. The facts given, both in regard to his miracles and his own private history, when touched upon, end so abruptly that much is left to the imagination of the reader, and is in that respect unsatisfactory. In all probability this has occurred because the Evangelists, when writing this history, thought principally of the then present generation, for whom it was especially designed, not fully appreciating the fact that this history, which they were endeavoring to record truthfully, would live and go on down through the centuries, gathering new strength and power as the years passed on. The people then living were supposed to know of the private surroundings and life of our Savior, and did not need to be told concerning them; but as age after age has passed, these particulars have been lost. It is for this reason, and because I would bring Christ nearer to all who read this, especially the young, that I have undertaken to write this possible story of Christ in the homes and among the people who had really learned to love him for even his human traits of character.

For instance, we read of the wonderful calling forth of Lazarus from the tomb, in which for four days he had lain; and we long to know in what manner this resurrection affected his life and that of the sisters he so loved. In the calling back to life of the little daughter of the ruler, Jairus, we find ourselves asking the question, "How did it affect the lives of her parents, and of the many friends around them? Did they become followers of the Christ because of this wonderful blessing conferred upon them, or did they allow their fears of the chief priests and scribes to make them hesitate in avowing what he had done?" When he cleansed the lepers, and healed the sick, and restored the blind, what did they do with the new life thus given to them? Did they spend it in his service, or in the questionable pleasures of the world? And when the terrible demoniac, from among the tombs in the country of the Gadarenes, was not only healed, but bidden to go and preach the gospel unto his benighted people, we long to know if he obeyed the divine injunction, and with what results.

I doubt not all these questions have occurred especially to the minds of young readers, who long to know more of this Jesus whom they too have learned to love; hence it has occurred to me that a story in which his possible life might be set forth, bringing out, and dwelling upon, the traits of character touched upon by the Evangelists, would make his personal life more real to us, and thus be a help, especially to the younger Bible students. In doing this I have adhered strictly to the Bible history as given of his life, only weaving in with it, to form a story, such other incidents as might be reasonably expected to approximate the unrecorded incidents of his life.

In my desire to make the human side of the Christ-life real to my young readers, I have in some instances enlarged upon the words of the Evangelists, but in no instance have I changed the ideas expressed by Christ, or in the slightest degree even modified the lessons he sought to inculcate on the contrary, I have endeavored to bring them within the comprehension of the youngest reader.

I have also endeavored, by the help of many Biblical writers, to give the incidents in consecutive order, which it seems the Evangelists sometimes failed to do, this making his life more of a biography from day to day, than mere disconnected incidents.

I have derived much help from Farrar's *Life of Christ*, Broadus' *Harmonies of the Gospel*, Wright's *Aids to Biblical Study*, and some others, for which I would make due acknowledgment.

Into my own life the writing of this narrative has brought a clearer, sweeter, closer companionship with Christ than I have ever known before; and my earnest prayer is, that it may bring this same blessedness into the lives of those who read it.

R. R. S.

"Oh! song of songs that grows sublime,
As onward roll the years,
Oh! story woven into rhyme
That melts the heart to tears!
I love, I love to hear that song!
It fills my soul with joy;
To Him all songs of praise belong,
Which mortal tongues employ.
Oh! sing that song to me again,
Whose charm doth never cease.
Of Him who died for sinful men—
Immanuel, Prince of Peace!"

~ Andrew Sherwood.

1

Why should'st thou fill today with sorrow
About tomorrow,
My heart?
One watches all with care most true.
Doubt not that
He will give thee, too,
Thy part.

~ Paul Fleming.

It was an old-fashioned, beautiful garden in the inner court of one of the finest houses in Capernaum. Two young people were amusing themselves together there; and, upon a rustic table within an arbor thickly overhung with vines and flowers, lay some odd games with which they had interested themselves. The day was yet young, and the dew lay heavy upon the dark leaves and flowers, and sparkled like diamonds in the sunshine just clearing the tops of the tall trees. The garden and palace belonged to Jairus, the chief ruler in the synagogue of Capernaum; and Miriam, a young girl of twelve, the maiden who was at this time in the garden, was his only and well-beloved child. Her companion, a youth of seventeen, was Marcus, the nephew of Jairus, who bestowed upon him all the affections and privileges of a son. Mary, the mother of Marcus, was the only sister of the ruler. Marcus had gone to live with his Uncle Jairus as his clerk, and was loved by him as a son.

Marcus and Miriam

Tell me again how you were injured said Marcus gently.

As the years passed, and the development of the boy advanced—as in those warm countries it does rapidly—Jairus found him possessed of unusual intelligence, and at the time our story opens, had for some months kept him near himself in the capacity of private secretary, or clerk. Between the two young people a warm affection existed, and the early morning hours, before the day had grown warm and sultry, were often spent by them together in the garden. Miriam was thoughtful and studious beyond her years, and not being strongly constituted, all outdoor amusements possible were encouraged by her parents in order to draw her mind from her studies and strengthen the frail body. Marcus never wearied of trying to entertain and amuse her. Just now the two stood together by the great sundial that was in the center of the garden, and were intently watching the shadow of the gnomon, as it crept slowly across the dial. A slave woman stood at a little distance from them, in whose dusky face shone tender solicitude for the young mistress, who was her especial charge.

"I sometimes find it hard to accept the story of King Hezekiah," said Marcus, watching intently the shadow on the dial.

Marcus and Miriam

"Marcus dear," said Miriam, gently interrupting him, "why do you say 'hard,' when you mean 'difficult'? That very mistake was treated of in my lesson yesterday."

"Ah, Miriam," said Marcus, somewhat impatiently, "why do you always drag your lessons into everything? When I come into the garden for an hour with you, I leave lessons and work and everything but pleasure behind me. I believe you never forget your studies for an instant."

"Oh, yes, I do," said Miriam, brightly. "But of what use will our studies be, what good will we derive from them, if we never apply what we have learned? Only this morning—"

"There, there, Miriam! Let us forget the lessons for the present. Your mind needs rest. I will say 'difficult' forever after," said Marcus gently, "if now, for this little hour, you will forget your studies."

"Very well, then," laughed Miriam. "I have at least done a little good, today. Now tell me what you were about to say of King Hezekiah, when I so unceremoniously interrupted you."

"I was about to say that it was 'difficult,'" with a merry glance at Miriam, "for me to realize how the shadow upon the dial could turn backward ten degrees, as Hezekiah desired it should. Forward it might have gone; but, unless the sun moved backward, how could the shadow do so? I do not want to question, but does it not seem almost incredible to you?"

"Yes," said Miriam, thoughtfully. "But, Marcus, what seems full of mystery to me, I simply do not question. I do not dare. There is so much in the books of the Prophets which I cannot understand, that if once I began to question, I would be lost in a labyrinth of doubt. We know they_ must be true, because they were inspired. Do we not?"

"Yes, I suppose we do," said Marcus, "but somehow, I lack the faith that accepts without question. I want to see a thing with my own eyes before I can fully believe and accept it."

"But that is not faith, Marcus. Faith is that which we believe without actually seeing, is it not?"

"I suppose so—yes," he answered, thoughtfully.

"I am sure I never could have lived if I had not always believed that someday I shall be well. I cannot know it, yet I have faith to believe it," said Miriam, gently.

"Do you believe it all of the time?" asked Marcus, eagerly.

"All of the time," answered the young girl.

"What reason have you for so believing? Did anyone ever tell you so?"

"No, I think not. I do not know why; yet, Marcus, when I was a tiny girl, during one of my severe attacks, I thought an angel stood beside me and said, 'Do not be afraid; I will save you'; and somehow, I am all the time expecting him."

"Dear little Miriam," said Marcus, gently stroking her thin hand, "tell me again how you were injured. Was it not when you were but a baby?"

"Yes, I was just a year old the day the accident happened. My nurse had started to carry me down the long flight of marble steps in the palace, when, upon the very top step, she slipped and fell the entire length, with me in her arms. She tried to save me, holding my head against her breast with her hands; but we were both taken up for dead at the foot of the stairs. She recovered, after a few weeks' suffering, hut some part of my spine was permanently injured. You know I have never been strong since, and suffer, at times, intensely."

"Yes, I know," said Marcus, still stroking the little hand. "Was it Ayeah?" he asked, in a low tone, indicating the nurse, with a motion of his head.

"Yes," whispered Miriam. "It nearly kills her to think of it. Low as we were speaking, she knows of what we are talking; she is devoted to me—poor Ayeah!"

The nurse had moved a few paces, and stood half turned away in the shadow of a great tree; but they saw that her head was bowed and her face wet with tears.

"My grandparents were determined she should be sent away, but my parents both knew that she was not to blame. She had nursed me from my birth with great care and tenderness, and it was an accident she could not have prevented. Some child had carelessly let fall the seed of a date, and she had trodden upon it and slipped. Anyone might have done the same. When she recovered consciousness, her grief was intense. She would drag herself from her bed and lie all night outside my door. My mother tells me that no persuasion or threats would move her, until she one day told Ayeah I needed her, and that she must soon get strong so as to help take care of me. After that she was as docile as a child, and soon grew strong enough to actually care for me again. Her devotion to me is very touching."

"She ought to love you, Miriam, not only for this accident, but because of your constant kindness to her. Where is a slave taught as you teach her, or shown such kindness and affection as you show her?"

"But Marcus, that is not all unselfish. I am not strong enough to have many young companions, so, of necessity, am thrown much upon

Ayeah for companionship while she attends upon me; and it is surely better to have her intelligent and possessed of some refinement than for me to be dependent upon an ignorant person for amusement. Besides, I like to teach her—it is good for me."

"Yes. you are right," said Marcus, looking upon the sweetly animated face with admiration. "But. Miriam, you are the most honestly truthful girl I ever knew. I believe you would tell the exact truth about anything, if you knew it would cost you your life."

"And would not you?" said Miriam, looking at him with eyes widely open in astonishment.

"Well," said Marcus, taken a little aback, "I am not so sure that I might not sometimes stop a moment to consider what was best in the matter."

"Oh, no, Marcus, you would not—I know you would not!" she answered eagerly.

They had returned to the arbor and were sitting together upon one of the rustic seats, and now a thoughtful silence fell between them for a moment, then Marcus said:

"Can you remember how the angel looked who came to you when you were so ill? What was he like?"

"No," said Miriam, "it is so long ago that I only remember he seemed a man, and yet I know he was an angel."

"Did you tell anyone at the time?"

"Yes, my mother. She said it was a beautiful dream sent to comfort me; that she and my father constantly prayed that God would heal me, as he did King Hezekiah. and she, too, believed that in time he would, but we must be patient and wait his time."

"Miriam," said Marcus, after another moment's thought, "have you heard them talking about Jesus the Nazarene?"

"The prophet of Nazareth?" questioned Miriam. "Yes, Abaron, my mother's body-servant when we travel, knows much about him, and I often hear my mother question him about the marvelous reports concerning this strange man. He once told her that there was a marriage feast in Cana, in the house where his brother was a servant; and that in the midst of the feast the wine gave out, and the family were greatly distressed and annoyed about it. The mother of this Jesus was there, and she went to her son and told him of the distress of the groom, who, I think, Abaron said, was in some way related to Jesus. Jesus ordered some large water jars filled at the well, and when this was done, he bade them draw from the jars and carry the water to the governor of the feast; and it was better wine than any they had hitherto had. Was not that wonderful?"

"It certainly was. I had not heard of this marriage feast, but of other things quite wonderful in many ways. I was talking only yesterday with James, the son of Zebedee, the master fisherman, and he told me some marvelous things that he had seen. One was, that as Jesus was speaking to a large multitude in the synagogue one Sabbath day, a demoniac rushed into the midst of the crowd, screaming and tossing his arms wildly about. Jesus said very sternly, in tones of command, as though speaking to someone hidden within the man, 'Come out of him!' and the poor wretch fell struggling and writhing upon the floor, crying out, 'I know Thee, the Holy One of God.' But soon he became quiet and arose, sane and well as any man. James said the people were so amazed that they quietly dispersed without a word; and it was all the more wonderful, since many had gone there simply to scoff and to deride the Nazarene.

"He also went into the house where Simon's wife's mother lay dangerously ill of a fever, and going to the bed, took her by the hand and said, 'Arise.' And she immediately arose from her bed as though wholly unconscious that she had been ill, and began to prepare the evening meal for the household.

"Many, many like things James told me, for he is much with Jesus. Miriam, why may not Jesus be the angel of your dream?"

"Perhaps he is," said Miriam, gently. "If he is, he will surely come."

Marcus looked, amazed at her simple trust. But it is ever such trust that brings the fulfillment of the promise: "They that wait upon the Lord shall renew their strength."

2

We take with solemn thankfulness
Our burden up, nor ask it less;
And count it joy that even we
May suffer, serve, or wait for
Thee, Whose will be done.

~ J.G. Whittier.

A long, hot day was drawing to a close in the city of Capernaum some months before the events narrated in the last chapter, and already the people were issuing from the overheated rooms below and emerging into the open air upon the flat roofs of the houses, in order to catch a breath of the cool breeze that now and then drifted over the city from the lake. Especially was this so among the humbler classes, whose houses were, for the most part, but one-story high, and became perfect ovens during the heat and glare of the noontide. On the flat roof of one of these humbler dwellings a young man sat, this evening, mending the fishing-nets that lay in a pile beside him. Now and again he would drop his work and his eyes would wander wistfully to the blue lake in the distance. He had a well-knit, manly frame, and an honest face, from which dark eyes looked almost solemnly out from beneath his dark hair. A woman sat a little way from him with an earthen dish of lentils in her lap, which she was preparing for the evening meal. As she worked, she furtively watched the countenance of her son, and once or twice, seemed on the point of speaking, but hesitated about disturbing his mood. A swallow darted across the low roof, and the youth's eyes, following it, encountered those of his mother, and were held by them. She spoke, then.

"What is it, James, my son?"

"I was thinking, mother, of the wonderful Nazarene."

"Hast thou again seen him?" she questioned. Yes, when thou didst send me to find my father's boat this morning for our usual allowance of fish; he was there."

"Tell me of him," she said, as he passed into thought.

"My father's boat was not at the mooring, but Simon was just landing. I sprang aboard and asked him, 'What luck?'

"'Not a single fish,' he answered, 'although we have toiled the entire night.'

"'That is hard. I wonder how father has fared,' I said.

"'Just the same. We left him still toiling with the nets when we weighed anchor, but not a fish. Thy brother John was with him.'

"Just then we heard a tumult, and looking, saw a large crowd coming down the beach, with Jesus a little in advance of them. As he reached the shore, the crowd pressed upon him, and stepping into the boat, he asked Simon to push out into the lake a little way. When he had done so, and had dropped the anchor, he sat down in the boat, facing the multitude, and talked to them. And oh, mother, such wonderful, gracious words as fell from his lips! I would, I could repeat them to you. The crowd pressed down to the water's edge, some even standing ankle deep in the water in order to be as near as possible to him. One poor fellow, with his right hand drawn into a knot, and both feet clubbed, waded out into the water, holding his maimed hand up to Jesus, and calling out piteously, 'Have mercy upon me, thou Jesus of Nazareth,' over and over again, until every heart was touched. But Jesus talked right on, apparently oblivious, until the man, in his great anguish of spirit to be healed, waded out beyond his depth, and beginning to sink, laid hold with his well hand upon the side of the boat, still keeping his eyes fixed steadily upon Jesus. The Master must secretly have noticed him before, for now, turning his eyes upon him, he said, 'Why thinkest thou that I am able to do this thing?' And the man, white with emotion, said, 'Because thy power is from God.' Then Jesus answered him:

"'Yes, from God alone such power is given; be it unto thee even as thou believest: go in peace.' As we looked we saw the crooked fingers unroll and the hand grow as supple and strong as its fellow; but when the man, in his gratitude, would have climbed into the boat to worship Jesus, he forbade him, saying:

"'Not so. Let your life show your gratitude to the Father for his mercy to you.' And, with a look of unutterable gratitude and joy, the man turned, and with a strong stroke, swam back to the shore; and the people crowded about him to look at the hands and the feet, aforetime so helpless and deformed, now straight and comely and ready to take up the work of life. And he was but one of the 'many who that day were healed.' While the multitude were thus diverted, Jesus said to Simon:

"'Push out now into the deep and let down thy net.' Simon answered him, 'Master, we have toiled all night and taken nothing; nevertheless, at thy word, I will let down the net.' So he threw his net from the boat, and almost immediately Jesus said, 'Now draw in.' Taking hold of the net, they all began to draw, but found it was already so heavy with fishes that they could not manage it alone. They beckoned to my father and John, who were in their boat, with myself and the servants, a little distance away. We went quickly, for our own boat was empty. With our assistance they soon, though with much difficulty, drew the nets to the surface, and we all began to fill the two boats with the finest fish I have ever seen. Soon both boats were full, and seemed in danger of sinking from the great weight; and still the nets were heavy with fish.

"Then we knew that divine power had interposed in our behalf, and we were amazed and almost terrified. Simon threw himself upon his knees at the Teacher's feet and cried out: 'Depart from me, Lord, for I am a sinful man, unworthy to have Thee bless me with Thy presence.' But Jesus only said gently, 'Fear not; henceforth thou shalt catch men.' From this I am sure he meant that Simon should help him to lead men into the better life of which he is so constantly telling us."

Here James stopped, and again his eyes turned wistfully to the deep blue waters of the Lake of Galilee. The mother's face was pale and wet with tears, but after watching her son intently for a few moments, she asked, very gently, "What more, my son?"

James started visibly, then answered in a low tone, which, though sad, seemed full of a suppressed, joy:

"He called me also, mother, to follow him! John I was sure he would call, because you can but see that he loves him, just as everyone who knows him must do; but me—so plain and quiet—he called me, too! What must I do?" with a slight hesitancy, as he asked the question.

The mother arose from her seat, unmindful of the dish of lentils she had been holding in her lap. and, approaching her son, knelt down beside him and took his hands into her own, bowing her head upon them. Her face was full of a holy awe, as though she had looked upon an angel as he passed. James leaned his forehead upon the bowed head of his mother, and each knew that the other was engaged in fervent prayer. Presently a footfall sounded in the court below, and they knew it was Zebedee, the father of James, taking care of the fish with which he had returned.

James raised his head and softly whispered:

"How can both John and I leave him alone with the boats and the nets? It was that that brought me home this evening. We have been all day with the Master upon the mountain, listening to his teachings to the people. How can I leave my father?"

"God will provide for that, my son. He who is honored with a call to follow the divine Master—for divine he surely is, else how could he have this strange power that can come alone from God?—he,! say, who is thus called, must never hesitate or look back. Your father hath his servants, and he is still a hale and sturdy man. Jesus, with his divine knowledge, would never have called thee to follow him. if he had seen that thy duty lay here. Our home will be lonely without our dear sons,"—and her lips quivered as she spoke—"but we. too, will love this divine teacher and rejoice that thou and thy brother are henceforth to be among his chosen and trusted companions. Besides, there will be intervals when we shall meet and know of that which concerns us both. Does your father know?"

"He was with us in the boat; and, when Jesus called to me, he bade me go."

"It will be well, it will be well," said the mother, slowly rising and laying her hands with a caressing touch upon the bowed head of her son, her eldest-born, her pride. Then she descended the stairs and went to join her husband.

3

Not till I loved Thee did I know Thee; nor till I knew Thee did I love Thee. I loved Thee first under the hazy veil of a faith that was but half faith; but when I came to know even what I know of Thee now, the love I had before, seemed unmeet to be called love; and yet it was that which lured me on to know Thee, and so to love Thee more.

~ William B. Philpot.

One beautiful dewy morning some weeks after the events narrated, Miriam sat in one of the arbors of the palace garden, her Ayeah crouched at her feet, looking up with intense interest into the face of her mistress. Miriam was telling her the ever-wonderful story of the sickness of Hezekiah, the visit of the prophet Isaiah, his message of death to the king, Hezekiah's prayer for recovery, and God's answer, wherein the king was granted fifteen additional years of life. When she told of the prophet's return to the king with God's gracious message, and of Hezekiah's demand for proof that the message was true by the shadow upon the sundial turning backward ten degrees, the dusky face of the nurse grew sober with thought, and finally she broke out, impetuously:

"How did he dare to ask for proof that God's message by the lips of the prophet was true? I wonder he was not smitten dead, or the promise at once recalled, for his lack of faith. The wonderful Nazarene teaches that only by faith in God's promises are they fulfilled. Hezekiah doubted instead. How could he then be healed?"

"The wonderful Nazarene, Ayeah—what knowest thou of him?" said Miriam, startled by having his name thus introduced by her nurse.

"Forgive me, little mistress," said the nurse, humbly, "but when thou didst last give me my day of holiday, Judith and I went over to the hills, where we had heard the Nazarene was to preach, and listened for ourselves to his gracious words. Was I wrong not to have asked thee first?"

"Yes, Ayeah, thou shouldest first have asked my permission; and I would not have withheld it, for I am greatly interested in him also. I will not reproach thee; but another time come first to me. How knowest thou but I might have asked thee to bear a message for me?" she answered kindly.

"Ah, sweet little mistress," said the nurse, kissing the white hand of the girl tenderly, "thou art always so kind and good, and thy Ayeah is so heedless. Tell me, my Miriam, dost thou believe he is the promised Christ?"

"I know not; I cannot say. I have not seen him. But he seems wonderful to me. Tell me about him, Ayeah. How did he seem to thee? What did he say? Oh, that I, myself, might see him!"

"Didst thou ever dream of an angel, my Miriam? If so, thou mayest know how fair and beautiful he is. I cannot describe him to thee, for I really did not think much about his appearance, so interested was I in what he was saying. He seemed everything lovely and good. He somehow made one forget for the time everything but just what he was talking about."

"And what did he talk about, nurse?"

"Well, he talked about the duty of people to each other, for one thing: exhorted servants to be obedient to their masters, and masters to be kind to their servants. He told us how our lives should always be pure and full of good works, and said little things were sometimes of great value in God's eyes, because they showed to him the true character of the heart. He said that people who professed to be righteous, yet sinned in their hearts, were like sepulchers that were white on the outside while the dead bodies were decaying within. While he was talking, a little toddling child ran up to him and took hold of his robe. A man standing near said to his mother, 'For shame! to let the child disturb the Teacher while he is speaking! Take it away.' But Jesus heard him, and stooping down, he lifted the little, laughing baby in his arms, and turning to the man, said, 'Except ye become as pure and innocent as this little child, ye cannot enter the kingdom of heaven.' And he held him in his arms while he talked, and the child played with his hair and cooed and crowed and looked up into his face, and once actually put up its little, rosy lips for him to kiss."

"And did he kiss him?" asked Miriam, breathlessly.

"Indeed he did! And when he saw some smiling at the act, he said, 'Let the little children come to me, and forbid them not; for of such is the kingdom of God.' And when he gave the sleeping baby to his mother—for he had at last nestled down on Jesus' shoulder and gone to sleep—many women pressed about him and held their children up tor him to bless. And 'he took them in his arms and blessed them.'"

"How beautiful!" said the young girl, musingly. Then, "And did he do anything wonderful—perform any miracles?" she asked.

The nurse hesitated a moment before she answered, half reluctantly:

"Little mistress, thy honored mother forbade my ever telling to thee anything that could in any way excite thee. I would rather say no more."

But Miriam smiled brightly as she said: "But, dear old Ayeah, it will excite me a great deal more to have thee disobey me than anything thou couldest tell me would do, and I command thee to tell me all thou didst see. Did Jesus perform any miracles?" As she saw the nurse still hesitate a little, she added sophistically, "I promise no blame shall attach to thee. I never would allow thee to disobey my mother—that would be wrong; but thou dost belong to me, and thou knowest she tells thee always to obey every command I give thee. Is it not true?"

"It is true, little mistress. I will tell thee all. He had performed many miracles before we reached there, they told us. He was speaking when we got there. But, as we were returning home, Jesus and a few people were walking quite a little in advance of the multitude, and Judith and I kept as near to them as we could, in order that we might hear as much as possible of what he was still saying to those with him, and also that we might escape the pressure of the multitude behind us. Presently, as we were hurrying forward, we saw, sitting by the wayside, the most wretched-looking object that I have ever seen. I have seen many lepers in my life, but this one was the most repulsive-looking man thou couldest imagine. He was almost blind and his body was badly distorted. As we approached, he was throwing dust upon his white head and crying out in a distressed voice, 'Unclean! Unclean!' Suddenly he saw Jesus and his companions approaching. He evidently had stationed himself by the wayside for that purpose, for he at once began to draw himself painfully forward until he fell prostrate at the feet of Jesus, crying in a beseeching voice:

"'Have mercy upon me, Lord! If thou wilt, thou canst make me clean!'

"Jesus stopped, and the look of tender pity and compassion that stole over his face, as he looked on this poor, outlawed creature, would surely have touched any heart. He looked searchingly into his face a brief instant, then reached forth his hand and touched him, saying, 'I will; be thou clean.' And instantly he was healed! The white, scaly skin disappeared; the colorless hair and eyebrows became black and glossy; the bent form stood erect and the knotted hands and feet grew supple and perfect. When he realized what had been done for him, he threw himself at the feet of Jesus and strove to clasp his knees, in his gratitude, crying reverently, 'Now know I thou art the Messiah.' But Jesus forbade him, saying, 'Go thy way; tell no man what God has done for thee, but take now thine offering, show thyself to the priest, and live henceforth for God alone.' And the man went away, leaping and singing and praising God. Little Miriam, thou art crying. What will thy mother say to thy Ayeah?" The good nurse's cheeks were also wet with happy tears as she finished her narrative, and Miriam whispered, "Oh, Ayeah, he is the Christ!"

At this moment Marcus entered the garden, and Miriam hastily dried her eyes, while the nurse, arising, seated herself on a stone bench a little apart from her young mistress. Marcus' manner betrayed suppressed excitement, and he at once began:

"Miriam, I have strange things to tell thee," but, as he seated himself beside her, he marked the agitation still apparent in her face, and he said, solicitously, "What distresseth thee, Miriam? Thou hast been weeping."

"Nay, Marcus, I was only affected by a touching story Ayeah was telling me," she answered sweetly.

"But Ayeah must not tell thee touching stories, my Miriam, if they cause thee to weep." he said, glancing reprovingly at the nurse.

"Nay, I will not have Ayeah blamed, Marcus I compelled her to tell me of the wonderful miracles done by the Nazarene."

"The Nazarene, Miriam! What knows Ayeah of the Nazarene? It was of him I came to tell thee."

Then at their request Ayeah had to repeat for Marcus all that she had told Miriam, he questioning her closely as to what she had seen and heard. Then he said:

"I, too, witnessed the healing of the leper, though I did not hear the discourse. Thy father, Miriam, kept me attending to some matters for him until I met the multitude returning as I went toward the hills. I was only a short distance behind the leper when he approached Jesus, and

I saw all that was done. Thou hast given a true account, Ayeah. It was wonderful, wonderful! And through it all I kept saying to myself, 'If he could do this for this wretched man, what could he not do for Miriam?' Dear Miriam, thou must see this Jesus—this wonderful Nazarene. I am sure that he would make thee strong and well."

"I long to see him," said the gentle maiden, "but not so much because he could give me strength—though that would indeed be glorious—as because I believe he is the Christ, the Holy One from God. Abaron has seen him many times, and I have heard him tell my mother that none but One inspired could talk as he doth. And more than once, Abaron says, he hath himself declared that he 'came forth from God,' and that whosoever believed he was the Son of God should have life eternal. What dost thou think of him, Marcus? How did he seem to thee?"

"I could only think, as I looked upon him, of the passage which we sometimes hear read in the synagogue: 'The chiefest among ten thousand, and the One altogether lovely.' He seemed to me a perfect type of a most perfect manhood. I cannot tell thee the color of his eyes—although I fancy they were a dark gray— but there was a depth of tenderness and love and compassion in them, as he looked upon thee, that made thee willing to lay thy very life at his feet. And his voice! Ah, Miriam, thou shouldest hear his voice! It reminded me of the sweet tones that steal from thy aeolian harp on a windy day—so wondrous sweet, yet with such a pathetic cadence as to make thee long to weep. It is as though he carried heavy sorrow in his heart that made itself felt through his most gracious words."

"Ah, Marcus, thou dost make me long more than ever to see him. Thinkest thou that my father would take me to him? I think that he regards him as almost divine; although our priests declare him blasphemous because he asserts so confidently that he and the Father are one. They would gladly compel us all to despise him if they could. Why are they so prejudiced against him, thinkest thou?"

"I know not. Possibly they are envious of his influence with the people."

"But why should that be, when all he says and does is to help and uplift them? Should they not rather learn of him and profit by his superior methods?"

"Guileless little Miriam!" said Marcus, with a smile, "thou hast yet to learn that priests are very human, and often fail to practice the charity they preach. But we will trust they cannot harm him, and will do our best to bring thee to his presence in some way."

"Where is he, Marcus?"

"Ah!" said Marcus, with a start of unpleasant remembrance. "At present he is not here. He felt constrained to remain without the city for a time, because our law condemns as unclean any who have touched a leper."

"But, Marcus, his touch healed and purified the leper. How could he, therefore, receive contamination therefrom? It seems to me that there could be no need of purification in his case."

"Yes, thou art right. Yet one of the remarkable things about the Nazarene is, that with all of his power, he yet scrupulously fulfills the requirements of the law. That is one thing that so incenses the Sanhedrin against him. So he has now evidently withdrawn himself from the city and his home, that they may not be able to say he did not fulfill the requirements of the law of purification. That accomplished, he will return; and then, my Miriam, thou must see him."

"Indeed, yes," she answered thoughtfully. At this moment a slave approached, and with respectful obeisance, said:

"Mistress Miriam, it is the hour for thy bath, and it is now prepared and waiting for thee."

"Yes, Sarah, we will come at once," said Miriam, rising and beckoning to Ayeah to accompany her. The maid came forward and threw a light scarf across the shoulders of the young girl, then drew back a step, respectfully, as Marcus said:

"I will go with thee as far as the entrance to the corridor, then I, too, will hasten to the bath, for I promised Antonius I would meet him in the public bath today, and it draws nigh the hour of our engagement."

When they reached the end of the garden, Marcus bent a moment gallantly over the hand of his little cousin, and said brightly:

"Until tomorrow. Miriam then relinquished her to the care of Ayeah, and turning, passed through the door into the outer court, and thence through a gateway into the narrow street.

4

They are slaves who fear to speak
For the fallen or the weak.
They are slaves who will not choose
Hatred, scoffing and abuse
Rather than in silence shrink
From the truth they needs must think;
They are slaves who dare not be
In the right with two or three.

~ James Russell Lowell.

As Marcus walked with a light step down the dusty way, many a passer-by turned and looked with admiring eyes after the handsome youth. Reaching the public bath, he passed along a wide corridor, with many entrances on either side, and entered a small apartment, one of many, and submitted himself to the hands of a slave, who rubbed and pummeled and douched him until his entire body was in a fine glow, then anointed him with fragrant oils and perfumes, and afterward handed him his own tunic for the public bath, or pool. Proceeding some distance further along the corridor, he pushed open a swinging door and entered a large apartment, or hall, in which the great pool lay. The walls of this apartment were elegantly frescoed with varied scenes of nymphs and satyrs bathing, with lofty palm trees and birds of gorgeous plumage and flowers of brilliant hues. Around the entire room ran a narrow balcony of marble, with luxurious couches and seats against the wall, and from this balcony, at short intervals, descended marble steps into the great basin, which was filled with perfumed water. Not many persons were in the pool when Marcus entered the hall, for the hour was somewhat early for those accustomed to frequent the place.

He paused for a moment on the balcony until he saw that his friend Antonius was already there, then he slowly descended one of the flights of steps into the water, motioning for one of the slaves to serve him wine upon one of the floating tables. All present greeted him with cordiality, and Antonius said, indicating a gentleman near him:

"I would present my friend Aurelius, of the household of Caiaphas, our high priest."

Marcus greeted him with dignity, at the same time taking mental note that something in his manner was not prepossessing. After the little flutter caused by the entrance of Marcus had subsided, Antonius spoke to a young man reclining in the bath at a little distance from them and said:

"Philip, we are all anxious to hear more of your wonderful story. Marcus will, I am sure, be interested."

"Undoubtedly," said Marcus, with a look of inquiry at Philip.

"It was only," said Philip, turning politely to Marcus, "a brief narration of my own experience with the prophet of Nazareth, in which the gentlemen were kind enough to be interested."

"He is no prophet!" said Aurelius, sneeringly.

"Go on! Go on!" cried all the others, with one accord.

Marcus gave a quick glance at Aurelius, and then one of inquiry at his friend Antonius; but nothing further was said, and Philip proceeded with his story.

"He may be no prophet—I am not here to argue that point—but he certainly is the most wonderful man I have ever chanced to meet."

"Prove it!" said Aurelius, with a half-concealed sneer.

Again Marcus looked at him, and something of the contempt he felt must have been visible in his face, for the lip of Aurelius curled scornfully.

"That will not be difficult to do," Philip calmly answered.

"Perhaps you are yourself one of his disciples?" queried Aurelius, contemptuously.

"The story! The story!" cried the others, tired of the delay; and Philip, taking up the broken thread of the narrative, ignoring the rude thrust, said quietly:

"It was the day after the wonderful cleansing of the leper, of which I have just told you, that, as I was leaving the city of Nain, whither I had gone late in the evening of the day before, I saw, just without the gates, a funeral procession moving slowly to the place of burial. Not wishing to disregard the amenities of life, I dropped behind until it should pass. It was one of the saddest sights I ever saw. A fellow traveler told me that the young man upon the bier was the sole dependence and comfort of his mother, a widow, who, by his death, was left alone and helpless. The poor woman, leaning heavily upon the arm of a kindly neighbor, followed close behind the bier, with bowed head and form convulsed with heavy weeping. Now and then she would raise her voice in the most pitiful lamentation: 'Oh, my son! My son!' And then the band of hired mourners, evidently thrilled and touched by her deep sorrow, would break forth into renewed and pitiful wailing, more real than is customary on such occasions.

"Suddenly I saw approaching from the way they went, the tall form of the Nazarene; and I, who had so recently witnessed the cleansing of the foul leper, wondered in my heart if he could restore life to the still form resting upon the bier. But no; I felt that were too much to believe, but he might say words that would comfort the stricken mother. He approached and touched the bier, and the bearers, either because they recognized him, or possibly to take an instant's rest, set it down, and the mother broke forth into renewed lamentations.

"Her sorrow seemed to appeal to Jesus, for, approaching her, he softly touched her uplifted hand and said, 'Weep not.' Then he bade them take the cloth from the face of the dead man; and, leaning over, he looked for a moment intently at the colorless face, then, touching the forehead gently with his finger, he said so distinctly that all could hear: 'Young man, arise.'

"I had pressed forward with the others, when we saw Jesus approach the bier; and now I saw the eyes open, like one suddenly aroused from sleep, and gaze with a startled look up into the face of Jesus. Then the young man sat up, and in an instant, taking the outstretched hand of Jesus, he stepped from the bier and stood upon his feet, exclaiming: 'Mother, I live!' And Jesus presented him to his mother alive.

"Then mother and son fell with great rejoicing upon each other's necks, and all the people sent up a shout of great joy; but when they turned and would have worshiped Jesus, he was gone, no man knew whither. Then the people who had passed so sorrowfully through the gates, turned and retraced their steps toward the city, the mother leaning joyously upon the arm of her restored boy, he walking with happy face and firm, elastic step beside her. A merchant from the city, who was present, threw his own tunic over the shoulders of the young man, and no one looking upon him would have believed that he had been carried dead through the gates of the city less than an hour before. Instead of the funeral chant and the wailing of the mourners, there arose a paean of triumph, a hymn of praise."

As Philip paused there was an instant of deep silence in the room, then many eager questions were asked and answered.

"Is not this the promised Messiah?" said one.

"He must have supernatural power," said another.

"Any sorcerer could have done the same! He is an impostor of the worst stamp, and should be taken care of by the authorities," said Aurelius, rising from his recumbent position in the bath.

"Then why," said Marcus, also rising, "should any die, if the sorcerers can restore life? That is a new doctrine to me. I also saw this man Jesus cleanse the leper, though I did not see him raise the dead; and I say, 'Woe unto him whose hand is raised against him, for his power is divine'!" And with a grave salute he passed up the marble steps and out of the room.

" Who is that arrogant fellow?" questioned Aurelius of Antonius.

"That," said Antonius, in surprise, "is Marcus, the nephew of the ruler of the synagogue, and a noble youth." At this, Aurelius looked annoyed, but only said: "You should have told me this in the beginning; this ruler is the very man I seek to conciliate, and I have begun by antagonizing the nephew."

Antonius made no answer, but in his heart, he thought, "No true gentleman would require to be told that he should treat all with courtesy."

Marcus hastened back to the palace of his uncle, after he left the baths, hoping that he might again see Miriam and tell her the story of the widow of Nain. But Ayeah met him with a sorrowful face and told him that her little mistress had been quite ill after her bath, and it was not permitted that anyone at present should see her; so he turned sadly away.

Marcus and Miriam

Woe unto him whose hand is raised against him!

He strolled aimlessly about the garden for half an hour or more, then determined to go direct to the father of Miriam and tell him all he had heard concerning Jesus, the wonderful Nazarene, and urge him to seek him and bring him at once to Miriam, that he might heal her also. He went to the private room in the official quarters of the ruler, and entered, as was his habit, unbidden. But no sooner was he within the room than he saw that his uncle was not alone, and he was about to withdraw when Jairus called to him. Turning to meet him, he saw to his surprise that Aurelius, the messenger of Caiaphas the high priest, was the ruler's guest.

Aurelius was visibly confused when he saw Marcus, but the two young men looked at each other as though they never had met before. Jairus presented them to each other, and then proceeded to say to Marcus (whom he had already begun to consult and trust in grave matters of business, seeing that he was endowed with rarely good judgment and keen insight into character, for one so young):

"The high priest, Caiaphas, has honored me by sending this, his trusted messenger, to consult with me concerning some disturbances that have arisen on religious questions."

"Nay, nay, my lord," interrupted Aurelius, hastily, "the difficulty has not arisen upon religious questions, but upon blasphemous utterances by one Jesus, whom the people of the lower classes regard as a prophet. He is a pestilent fellow, given to stirring up strife, and the high priest would fain have an example made of him."

Jairus held up his hand to enjoin silence, for, glancing at the face of his nephew, he beheld it flushed with excitement and the eyes ablaze with suppressed anger. "You may say to the most honorable Caiaphas for me that I have already made much inquiry concerning the Nazarene, at the request of the most honorable Annas, the father-in-law of Caiaphas, and thus far I discover nothing for which he could be held amenable to the law."

"He is blasphemous," broke in Aurelius, impetuously.

Again Jairus held up his hand to enjoin silence, and continued: "But I will pursue my inquiries diligently until convinced either of his innocence or guilt. You may bear to our honorable high priest our expressions of profound respect and our regret that we cannot more fully coincide with his views in this matter." Then Jairus arose to signify that the audience was at an end; and Aurelius, flushed and confused, bowed low and hurriedly retired. Marcus had remained standing during the entire interview, but had spoken no word. Now his uncle said to him, as he threw himself upon a couch: "Thou dost not seem to feel much honored by the visit of the courteous Aurelius."

"His heart is as black as the dead coals on the altar. Mark me, he is plotting, for some end of his own, to destroy this wonderful prophet."

"Thou hast seen him before?" questioned his uncle.

"Yes, only an hour ago;" and he narrated the scene at the public bath.

Jairus seemed much interested and impressed by all he heard, and when Marcus concluded, he said to him:

"And thou? What thinkest thou of Him?" Marcus, again rising to his feet, said, with uplifted hand:

"He is the Messiah the prophets have foretold. His is the Christ, the Holy One of God!"

"What reasons hast thou for thinking thus, other than those thou hast given?" queried the ruler.

Then Marcus told him what he himself had seen in the cleansing of the leper, and what James had told him of the things that he himself had seen—of the miraculous draught of fishes, of the instantaneous healing of Simon's wife's mother, and many other things of like nature. When he had concluded, his uncle said: "I think thou must be right, my son such marvelous power could come alone from God. We must beware how we cross swords with such a power, or hold in low esteem one whose origin seems truly to be divine."

Then Marcus said: "Oh, my father, why do we not seek him for the healing of our dear Miriam? Even now, the nurse tells me, she lies very ill, and one word from this man would give to her the strength she never has possessed. May I not go forth, and finding him, bring him at once to you for her sake?"

"Alas, my dear Marcus! I have not been unmindful of the welfare of the child so dear to us all, and as soon as she was taken ill, I sent Abaron, who knows well the prophet by sight, to beseech him to come to us. But he soon returned to say that at daylight this morning, Jesus, with several of his disciples, left in a boat to go to the country of the Gadarenes, I suppose to preach his gospel to that benighted people. I much fear they will not listen to him; but be that as it may, we cannot now find him to entreat him for Miriam. But do not be troubled now for her, for only a moment before you came, her mother sent me word that the violence of the attack was passing, and she had fallen into a tranquil sleep. The danger has for the present passed, and before another attack I trust we shall have found the teacher, and entreated him for her recovery. She could not be dearer to your heart, my son, than she is to ours. Be comforted."

And laying his hand a moment kindly upon the arm of the young man, he passed into the more public quarters of the building. Marcus was very fond of his young cousin Miriam, and there was a double bond between them, because they had in early childhood been betrothed to each other by their parents, which was not an uncommon event in that country. As Miriam grew to womanhood she had developed a most beautiful character, and was well beloved by all who knew her. I say to womanhood, because, although Miriam was still only about twelve years of age, in that hot climate where plants and shrubs shoot up with great rapidity into perfection, so also do children early arrive at maturity, at an age when in our colder atmosphere they would still be looked upon as children of tender years. I cannot better illustrate this, than by quoting direct from one of our most learned writers. He says:

"The age of twelve years was a critical age for a Jewish boy. It was the age at which, according to Jewish legend, Moses had left the house of Pharaoh's daughter; and Samuel had heard the voice which summoned him to the prophetic office; and Solomon had given the judgment which first revealed his possession of wisdom; and Josiah had first dreamed of his great reform. At this age a boy, of whatever rank, was obliged, by the injunction of the rabbis and the custom of his nation, to learn a trade for his own support. At this age he was so far emancipated from parental authority, that his parents could no longer sell him as a slave. At this age he became a *ben hat-torah*, or 'Son of the Law.' Up to this age he was called '*Katon*,' or little; henceforth he was '*gadoi*,' or grown-up, and was treated more as a man; henceforth, too, he began to wear the '*tephillin*,' or 'phylacteries,' and was presented by his father, in the synagogue, on a Sabbath, which was called from this circumstance the '*shahhath tephillin*.'

"This period, too, the completion of the twelfth year, formed a decisive epoch in a Jewish boy's education. According to Juda Ben Tema, at five he was to study the Scriptures; at ten, the Mishna; at thirteen, the Talmud; at eighteen, he was to marry; at twenty, acquire riches; at thirty, strength; at forty, prudence. Nor must we forget that the Hebrew race, and Orientals generally, develop with a precocity unknown among ourselves, and that boys of this age (twelve years), according to Josephus, could and did fight in battle; and that, to the great detriment of the race, it is to this day regarded as a marriageable age among the Jews of Palestine and Asia Minor."

These facts are in many respects true of both sexes, especially so as to the marriageable age. In the Orient, especially in India, little girls of tender years are often married to men sometimes old enough to be their grandfathers, and many are the hardships they endure on account of this unholy custom. In the case of Miriam, her parents, both already tasting of the true gospel of Christ, protected their little daughter from many things to which she otherwise would have been subjected, and helped the beautiful development of her character; so that, although in her childhood she was betrothed to her cousin, their marriage was not expected to be consummated until her health at least should be permanently established. She had been taken to many physicians and subjected to much painful treatment, which, alas! thus far had been of no benefit whatever, the attacks returning each time with renewed violence, until all felt that her delicate frame could not much longer resist the dreadful suffering thus entailed. So it had come to pass that in her present suffering they had sought to find Jesus, the wonderful Nazarene, but learned to their sorrow that he had left Capernaum to go into the benighted country of the Gadarenes.

5

Bassanio: "For thy three thousand ducats here is six."
Shylock: "If every ducat in six
thousand ducats were in six parts, and
every part a ducat, I would not draw them; I would have my
bond."

~ Merchant of Venice.

In one of the narrow streets of the older portion of the city, Joseph Armenta, an industrious mechanic, and his wife Sarah, lived with their little family of four healthy children. By the most rigid economy these two honest people had been able to purchase the tiny house and garden, and after years of hard toil had paid for it, with the exception of a small mortgage held by a moneylender. This they confidently expected to lift before the year should close; and they would then own their home free of all encumbrance. But a scourge of fever of a malignant type passed through the city of Capernaum, and soon Joseph Armenta and his two younger children were stricken and died with the disease. Young Joseph, the eldest child, was the first to be prostrated by it, but having a strong and vigorous constitution, he rallied, and at the time of his father's death, was able, though still weak, to stand with his mother at his father's bedside and receive his last words.

"Wife," said the dying man, "thou must be brave for the sake of Joseph and little Ruth, who are still left to thee. Life is very sweet, but it is God's will; we must not murmur. Joseph"—turning his eyes upon his son—"will take my place and help thee with thy burdens. The money for the last claim, all but a few gold shekels, is in the secret place of which thou knowest. The claim is now due, and but for this fatal illness, I should be able to pay it. Abrams knows this, and will not be hard on thee, my wife, but will wait a little, I doubt not."

Then he closed his eyes wearily and opened them no more on earth. The poor wife, stricken and worn with grief, was an easy prey to the disease that even then had laid its heavy hand upon her, and very soon was laid beside the husband and children she loved, in the silent city of the dead.

"Take good care of little Ruth," she whispered to her son at the last; "thou knowest what thy. Thy old Aunt Eunice will give up her own house and come and live with thee. She has promised, and thou, my good son, will be obedient and good to her as thou hast ever been to me." Then, with a loving look at the doubly orphaned children, she closed her eyes and died.

But alas! the hearts of men, closed to God's love, are ofttimes pitiless. The Jew, Abrams, had long coveted the neat though humble home of Joseph Armenta for his own dwelling, and now, when by strict interpretation of the law, he could seize it, he was not slow to embrace the opportunity. Returning, sorrowful and weak, from his mother's funeral, Joseph found him in possession of the house, and the lad was told that he and his sister could not lodge there even for that night, though the day was already far spent. In vain Joseph told him of his father's last words and pleaded for a few days of grace.

"I will indeed pay thee, if thou wilt only wait," he urged, with not unmanly tears. "It is the only home we have, my little sister and I, and our parents told us to stay herein."

But Abrams only laughed as he said: "Nay, my lad, it is thy home no longer, but mine. Thy father was an honest man, and would not wish me to be robbed of my just claim."

"But I will pay thee soon the little due thee."

"Show me now thy gold," the old man said greedily.

But this Joseph was afraid to do, lest he should lose that also, so he only said:

"I cannot, today."

"Then get thee gone!" the old man said angrily. "And see that thou touchest nothing in this house but thine own and thy sister's raiment; all else is mine."

"May I not take my bed?"

"Begone!" said the Jew. "One moment more of tarrying and thou shalt take not even thy raiment!"

So Joseph, seeing that further argument was vain, went hastily into the inner room, and while hurriedly gathering together his own and his sister's scanty wardrobe into a small bundle, failed not to draw from its concealment and hide in his bosom the tiny purse of gold that now was his sole inheritance. He did this none too soon, for Abrams came into the room and watched him narrowly, as though to see that nothing was concealed. Joseph's heart trembled lest he should offer to search him; but this he did not, contenting himself with saying sharply:

"There! Thou hast enough," and motioning him the door.

Upon the threshold, Joseph turned and looked with longing eyes around the rooms so dear to him, clothed with so many sacred memories, the only home he could remember, the place where his beloved parents had died. Then he turned to the old man, still narrowly watching him, and said:

"The God of the fatherless will reward thee. Thy bed beneath this roof will not be one of peace!"

The old man raised his arm as though to strike him, but Joseph, turning, ran from the house and hastened to the home of his Aunt Eunice, where she and little Ruth had gone to prepare for her removal to their home. The aunt stood aghast as Joseph told his impassioned tale; but she was a God-fearing woman, so when he had ceased and she had asked a few earnest questions, she said:

"God's will be done, my son. It is not as we have planned, but we may not murmur. The man has the law upon his side, and there is no mercy in his heart. We are poor and have no friends who can relieve us; we must take up the burden as best we can. Thou and thy sister must stay here; I am thy next of kin. These two little rooms are mine and thine, but whence food is to come for three, I know not. I manage to earn a little day by day, but often I have gone hungry to my bed. How can I feed you also, my poor children?"

"My dear aunt," said the boy, stoutly, "am I to be a burden upon thee? Not so; my hands shall earn enough for all of us. Thou and my little sister shall keep the house, while I blow the furnace, as of old, in the great brass foundry where my father worked. When my father died the master workman promised I should have my place as soon as I was able to work again."

"God bless thee, lad!" said his aunt, fervently. "Thou hast not yet the strength for work, but He who sent the ravens to Elijah will not leave us comfortless."

With a sudden recollection Joseph thrust his hand into his bosom and drew forth the precious purse, and pressing it into the hand of his aunt, said:

"So doth He even now provide." Then, as she looked in speechless astonishment at the gold within her hand, Joseph told how he had secured it and concealed it from the pitiless Abrams.

"Now God indeed be praised!" said the good woman. "Yes, this was truly thine. Abrams had no right to this when he took thy home. Thou hast a clear head, Joseph, as well as an honest hand."

So it came to pass that the three took up their life together with thankful hearts, and very soon Joseph returned to his old place in the brass foundry, where his father had worked for many years before his death.

6

God doth not need
Either man's works or his own gifts; who best
Bear his mild yoke, they serve him best; his state
Is kingly; thousands at his bidding speed,
And post o'er land and ocean without rest:
They also serve who only stand and wait.

~ John Milton.

The heat from the great furnace proved too much for Joseph's eyes, already greatly weakened by his severe illness, and they soon began to inflame. His nights were full of suffering from them, but he was a brave young fellow and would not yield to the pain. He still kept on, week after week, with his work uncomplainingly. At last, one day when the heat was unusually severe, he fell prostrate, and was raised by his companions, insensible. They carried him to the outer air; but when they had brought him back to consciousness his sight was gone—he could see nothing. For several days he lay in a darkened room bemoaning his sad lot; but his hot tears only intensified his suffering, and his bitter lamenting wrung the hearts of his sister and aunt. At length the foreman of the foundry, who had become much attached to Joseph, himself took him to one of the most eminent surgeons in the city, who examined the poor eyes carefully, then shook his head sadly at the foreman, and privately told him the boy would never see again.

To Joseph he said: "Use this lotion till the inflammation abates, then we can tell better what you need."

A drunken horseman came thundering madly along.

The inflammation in the lids in time abated, but they opened not to the light again.

As the weeks passed and the kind foreman ceased to visit his little friend, Joseph knew without words that his case was hopeless, and tried to accept bravely what he felt to be inevitable. But this was not so easy, when he thought of his aunt and little Ruth deprived of his assistance as a breadwinner. Then he almost rebelled. One day he said bitterly:

"I cannot see God's justice in letting my good parents die, and their children suffer thus, and men like the money-lending Abrams live and prosper."

"Hush, hush, my son!" said his aunt. "God will show forth his glory, sooner or later. Only be patient and bide his time."

"Ah, yes," said the boy, a little less bitterly, "but where is the bread to come from in the meanwhile?"

"There are still ravens," said his aunt, reverently.

"I have thought of a way, brother Joseph," said little Ruth, creeping up lovingly into his arms, as he sat brooding sorrowfully.

"Thou hast, little one?" said Joseph, smiling as he drew the dainty figure up to his heart. "And what is thy way? May we hear it?"

"Why, surely," said the child. "I am to go with thee to the gates of the synagogue every day; surely, many will pity thy blindness."

"Turn beggar!" said Joseph, bitterly.

"Nay," said little Ruth, eagerly, "thou art to do nothing but sit beside me at the gate. Even I will not ask alms, but when I see a kind face turned toward us, I will just hold out my little red cap, and surely many will drop a mite therein."

The lad saw, in imagination, the little sunny head his mother had so loved, the pretty, upturned face, and the extended hand with the crimson cap therein, and it was more than the overwrought nerves could bear. He broke into convulsive sobs, as he pressed the little sister to his heart. Frightened at his violent weeping, she whispered:

"But, Joseph, we will not go if thou dost not wish to. Only what will Aunt Eunice do for our daily bread?"

Her unselfishness brought back his self-control, and kissing her, he said quietly:

"Yes, we must help Aunt Eunice, dear. Thy plan is a good one. Shall we go at once?" For it was still early in the day.

"Oh, shall we?" said Ruth, starting up eagerly and running to fetch her cap.

She kissed her aunt goodbye, and taking her brother's hand, walked with him the short distance that lay between their home and the synagogue. They found a shady seat in the shadow of the gate; and Ruth's plan worked even better than she hoped, for many were the coins dropped in the little cap held out so mutely, yet so appealingly, to the passers-by.

Day after day they could be seen in the same place, and evening after evening found many coins in the crimson cap. But one evening, about two weeks after they first started out thus together, as they were crossing one of the narrow streets on their return home, a drunken horseman came thundering madly along, and everyone sought to escape his plunging horse, infuriated by the master's whip and spur. Someone seized Joseph and dragged him out of harm's way, and trembling in every limb and with a great dread at his heart, he cried aloud:

"Ruth! Ruth! Oh, where is my little sister?'

The thundering hoofs had passed on down the street, and Joseph grew cold with fear as she did not answer him. Then he heard someone near him say softly:

"Had he not better be told?"

He turned almost fiercely in the direction of the speakers, crying out:

"Tell me the worst at once! Is she dead?"

"Nay, nay; she hath only swooned. The hoof of the great horse struck her back, but she will soon be all right. We have a litter to carry her home upon, and thou canst walk beside and hold her hand, if thou wilt."

Greatly relieved, Joseph begged to be taken to his sister, and bending over her, called her by all endearing names; but for once her ear was deaf to the voice she so loved. Joseph walked sadly by the litter, holding the hand of the inanimate maiden.

Results proved that the great hoof had struck the delicate spine and so injured it that the lower limbs would be paralyzed for life. Joseph's grief was terrible at learning this, and he blamed himself ceaselessly forever taking her out to the street, when unable to protect her. But as Ruth grew better she seemed to have matured with the suffering, and she tried ceaselessly to make her brother feel that they should be thankful that they were not both killed: that God had permitted this accident for some wise purpose, which some day he would let them understand. But Joseph could not feel reconciled, and sat depressed and silent most of the time.

One day Ruth said to him: "Dost thou not see, my Joseph, how now, when there are two of us to claim pity, my little cap will be doubly heavy at night? Thou hast only to carry me in thy strong arms to the gate of the synagogue, for I can direct thy steps as well from thine arms as though I walked beside thee."

"Dost think I ever will let thee go upon the street again in thy helplessness, to be a spectacle for curious eyes?" asked Joseph, almost fiercely. But little Ruth only patted his hand lovingly and answered him:

"I know thy kind heart too well, my Joseph, to believe thou wouldest deny me the sunshine because of a foolish fear. I am counting the hours till thou wilt take me forth again."

"On to the doorstep, or under the shadow of this house wall, yes; but never to the synagogue again, my sister."

"And Aunt Eunice may toil from day to day to keep us in idleness," was Ruth's low-spoken answer.

Joseph had no reply for this; the thought was the sorrow of his life, yet he could see no way to remedy the evil except the one— to him abhorrent—course suggested by his sister.

Ruth grew stronger from day to day, but to all it was apparent she would never walk again. Joseph now daily carried her out in the cool of the morning and evening, and sat with her in the shadow of the house, or oftener still carried her up upon the flat roof of the little house, after the violent heat of the day had passed. One evening as they were silting thus, Joseph recounting the stories his mother had told him in his childhood for the entertainment of his sister, their aunt approached them with suppressed excitement in her manner.

"What is it, Aunt Eunice?" asked little Ruth, seeing instinctively that something more than usual had occurred to excite her.

"Oh, my children!" she answered, approaching Joseph and laying a hand tenderly upon his shoulder, "never question again the wisdom and justice of God, or doubt his care for the oppressed. He metes out punishment and reward, as his wisdom sees is best."

"What is it, aunt?" asked Joseph, awed by her manner.

"Last night the little home of thy father, that we all so loved, was burned by fire, and Abrams not only lost all that he possessed, but was himself so injured while trying to save his property that even if he survives his injuries, he will be blind for life."

Joseph, greatly excited, had arisen to his feet, and now cried earnestly: "God forgive me for the curse I pronounced upon him! God does recompense the evil-doer. Knowest thou how it came to pass?"

"None know, not even the man himself. He was aroused from slumber by someone pounding on his door and calling him. The whole house was burning when he awakened. He was so frightened and bewildered that he rushed out into the street before he thought of his money. He had been in the habit of taking his money and valuables home with him every night and hiding them in his own room for safety; and now he ran again into the burning house to secure them. What happened while he was there none know. Abrams says two men followed him into the house, and after he had secured his bag of money, knocked him down. The neighbors found him helpless on the floor of his room, his clothes all ablaze. They dragged him out and did everything possible for him, but he is crippled for life, even should he live, and penniless."

"How much better off we are, after all, than he!" said Ruth.

A few mornings after this, Ruth saw that a deeper shade of care was on the face of her aunt, and urged her lovingly to tell the cause. After some hesitation she said:

"My dear children, it is wrong to trouble your young hearts, but I have spent my last mite for our breakfast, and know not whence the next meal is to come." And the tears began to flow over her face.

"Is that all?" said little Ruth, cheerily. "We will bring home my little cap full of coins today, will we not, Joseph? It needed something to make us go. We have been idle long enough, and I am longing for the sunshine once more."

"Yes, come," said Joseph, rising. "Get her ready, Aunt Eunice, and I will carry her forth."

He felt he could resist no longer, and when his aunt said fervently, "God bless you both, my children; you have lifted a heavy burden off my heart," he knew that he was right. Ruth was in an ecstasy of delight, and while her aunt prepared her for the walk, chattered incessantly.

"Who knows but the blessed prophet of Nazareth may heal the eyes of our Joseph, as he did the eyes of the blind man by the wayside, of whom you told us yesterday?" said Ruth. "Oh, would it not be glorious to have our Joseph see again! Does he really do all the wonderful things the people tell of him?"

"I think he does, Ruth. He must be good, and have this wonderful power from God. I would myself love to see him," said the good aunt.

"I shall watch for him as he goes to the synagogue," said Ruth, eagerly, "and beg him to heal Joseph. He will pass close to us as he goes through the gate. Perhaps he may come today—who knows? Oh, hurry, brother! let us go at once!"

"Place her upon my arm, cushion and all," said Joseph, to his aunt. He was visibly touched by the conversation. Could this Jesus, of whom he had heard so much, really heal him as he had healed others? It seemed more than he could believe.

Ruth guided him very skillfully from her seat on his arm, and they were soon in their old place in the shadow of the gate. Joseph placed the cushion he had brought so as to make her as comfortable as possible, and the pathetic picture the two formed, sitting in their helplessness side by side, touched all hearts and brought many coins into the little cap.

"I am afraid the prophet will not come today," said Ruth, as the shadows began to lengthen. "But he will come to us before many days; I am sure he will."

"You are tired, little sister; I must take you home."

"I think I am hungry," said Ruth, pathetically; "we did not have a very sumptuous breakfast. But will we not have a good supper?" she asked, triumphantly, as she made Joseph feel the weight of the little cap. She placed the coins in the leather pouch, usually quite empty, that Joseph carried concealed in his tunic; and putting the cap upon her head, Joseph lifted her in his arms, and they were soon safely at home, to the relief and joy of their aunt.

7

Be not o'ermastered by thy pain,
But cling to God: thou shalt not fall;
The floods sweep over thee in vain,
Thou yet shalt rise above them all:
For when thy trial seems too hard to bear,
Lo! God thy King hath granted all thy prayer:
Be thou content.

~ P. Gerhardt.

Day after day found the brother and sister in the same place, and day after day God touched the hearts of the people, so that they never returned empty-handed. But little Ruth watched in vain for the coming of the great prophet who was to restore her brother's sight. Her faith grew stronger as the days passed. If only he would come, she was sure that he would be pitiful and heal her brother. But Jesus had gone into the hill country to teach the people there and heal their sufferings. This, Ruth could not know, as day by day she strained her eyes looking down the narrow street to catch the first glimpse of his coming, and praying in her trusting little heart that God would send him to them. She had ceased to talk about him, but she watched and prayed the more; and no one ever waited and trusted in the Lord in vain.

One day the heat was unusually great even for that warm country, and Joseph and Ruth were early in their places by the gate in order to avoid walking in the hot sunshine later in the day. The air was sultry and oppressive, and the Lake of Galilee, in the near distance, showed not even a ripple upon the bosom of its waters. As the hours passed and the heated atmosphere grew more and more oppressive, even Ruth, with her vivacious, cheery temperament, grew languid and depressed, and finally said to her brother:

"I am so tired, Joseph. Dost thou not think we might go home? The people have been very kind today, and already many coins are in the little cap."

Joseph's heart was instantly on the alert for fear of ill to his sister, and he asked anxiously: "Art ill, my little Ruth? Has the pain returned then to thy head or thy spine?"

"Nay, nay; I am not ill," she answered quickly. "Only the heat is so oppressive that even the trees seem to dance before my eyes and the houses to sway, and I am so tired of watching for— Oh, why does he delay!" and tears trickled slowly down the pale cheeks of the girl. These Joseph could not see, but he feared, from her words and her languid voice, that she was really ill.

"Come, dearest, we will go at once," he said, making ready to rise.

At that moment a murmur as of many voices in glad chorus fell on their ears and the tramp of many feet approaching them.

"Hark! hark!" said Ruth, breathlessly, laying her hand on Joseph's arm to detain him. "Dost thou not hear? Oh, Joseph, he is coming! At last he is coming!" She raised herself as far as she could in her helpless condition and looked wistfully down the street.

"Yes, yes, it is he! I see him plainly now; and many others are with him. They are coming directly toward the gate. Oh, Joseph, he is looking at us! He is here!"

It was indeed Jesus, and his heart was filled with compassion as he looked upon the two helpless children. Ruth had framed many pretty speeches in her childish heart that she would make to him, pleading for the restoration of her brother's eyes, when he should come; but now that he was actually standing before them—for he had stopped beside them— she could only stretch out one thin little hand to him appealingly, while the other rested on her brother's shoulder, and falter out pathetically, with her sweet, flower-like face uplifted: "Teacher! My brother! He—is—blind!" Joseph had grown very white, even to the lips, with emotion, when he heard that the wonderful prophet of Nazareth was really beside them; and he, too, lifted his face with its sightless eyes to where he felt the prophet stood, and his lips moved as if in prayer; but no one except Jesus heard the plea he uttered: "My little sister, teacher—heal her, heal her!" Jesus leaned over and looked earnestly into the face of the blind boy, then he laid a hand tenderly on each young head, and said softly but impressively:

"According to your faith be it unto you!"

He had no need to ask them of their belief; faith in his power was stamped on each young face. As the impressive words were spoken, Joseph opened his eyes, so long closed to the light, and the first object his restored vision caught was the face of Jesus, as it bent tenderly above him; and that remained indelibly impressed upon his heart. Ruth had kept her eyes fixed upon her brother's face from the moment Jesus bent over him, and now, when she saw his eyes open and look up intelligently into his face, she sprang joyously to her feet, and throwing her arms about his neck in rapture, cried:

"Thou dost see, my Joseph! Thou dost see! Thanks be to God and his prophet!"

Joseph held her close to his heart and faltered, "And thou, my little sister, thou, too, art healed!"

And then for the first time Ruth realized that she was using her paralyzed limbs as freely as in her childhood. In her joy over her brother's recovery she had not once thought of herself, but, as often follows unselfish devotion, she found that the blessing had also fallen upon her own head.

"Oh, let us find and worship him!" she cried.

But when, after this instant of almost delirious joy, they turned to seek him "he had passed through their midst" and disappeared.

"Oh, Joseph, we must find him!" little Ruth cried. And someone pointing down a narrow street as the way the prophet had gone, they hastened, hand-in-hand, that way, hoping to overtake him and pour forth their gratitude.

They hurried joyously on, Joseph walking with firm, true step and with head erect, while Ruth danced happily beside him, all languor and depression gone, and all thought of the oppressive heat forgotten.

Marcus, the nephew of Jairus, in passing to and from the synagogue, had become much interested in the two unfortunate children who daily sat in the shadow of the gate, and more than one coin had found its way from his hand into the little cap of Ruth. He soon saw they were no common mendicants, and little by little, had drawn their sad history from them. He providentially chanced—if such a phrase may be allowed—to be passing at the time of their miraculous healing, and witnessed it all with a sympathetic heart. He also wanted to find the Christ, as he now firmly believed Jesus to be, on Miriam's account; so he, too, was greatly disappointed that he had so quietly and quickly disappeared during the brief instant of their first great joy. Seeing Joseph and Ruth start on the search for him, he followed closely after them, so that if they found him, he, too, could make his plea.

As the children hurried on, they saw a man, decrepit and blind, sitting near the gateway of a large mansion, holding his mendicant's cap despondently in his hand. The children's hearts, so full of gratitude and joy, were filled with pity, and they paused as though they would speak to him. Marcus drew near and whispered in Joseph's ear, "It is Abrams, who robbed your dead father." Joseph drew back an instant, then, reaching for the little cap, still in Ruth's hand, he emptied the entire contents into the old man's cap, and hastened on.

Hearing the unusual rattle of coin in his cap, the beggar called out excitedly:

"Who art thou who so bounteously rememberest the unfortunate?" Then as the echo of receding footsteps alone reached his ear, he called after Joseph:

"The God of Israel multiply thy blessings day by day for evermore."

Marcus bent and whispered: "Thy benefactor is the lad Joseph, whom thou didst rob of home and all the comforts of life, and whose sight has just been restored by the prophet of Nazareth. His gift to thee is the gratitude of his heart for God's great mercy to him."

"Eh? What sayest thou? Joseph's sight restored? Now God be merciful to me a sinner!" And the old man's head sank despondently upon his breast. But Marcus noted that his hand, through it all, clutched tightly the cap that contained the coin. His avaricious heart could rise no higher! Of such it has been said, "He is joined to his idols, let him alone."

8

> Thou art my King,
> My King henceforth alone;
> And I, thy servant, Lord, am all thine own.
> Give me thy strength.
> Oh, let thy dwelling be
> In this poor heart that pants, my Lord, for thee!
>
> ~ Tersteegen.

When Joseph and Ruth found that it was impossible for them at that time to find Jesus, they turned from the more public street upon which they had been walking, and hastened down a narrow side-street that brought them to their own home. They could scarcely wait, in their eagerness to show their aunt what had been done for them. They had left her that morning, the one a hopeless cripple, the other blind for life; they return to her well and strong! What could she say? Marcus had hastened after them, and reached the open door in time to see the rapturous delight of their old aunt, and her almost incredulous surprise at the restoration of her two dearly loved children.

"Joseph," she would repeat again and again, "canst thou truly see me?"

"Yes, aunt, as well as I ever saw thee in my life."

"Now God be praised! And my little Ruth on her own feet again! Child, let me see thee walk."

"Wouldest see me dance?" said Ruth, merrily, dancing about the floor with graceful curves and bows, as she had seen the singing girls do on the public feast days.

"My children, let us thank God for his wonderful mercy to us." And dropping upon their knees, she threw her arms about the two and poured forth a fervent prayer of thanksgiving and praise, while tears and sobs choked her utterance. Marcus withdrew to a little distance, till their outburst of grateful joy had in a measure subsided, then he again approached the open door. Ruth was the first to see him, and darted forward, crying:

"Oh, Aunt Eunice, this is my good young man!" and drew him to her aunt's side, where she recounted, to his no small embarrassment, his many acts of kindness when she had sat beside the gate of the synagogue. He found the aunt, a plain but intelligent woman, and together they all talked over the wonderful events of the morning.

"To think I am no longer blind!" said Joseph, pacing the room excitedly. "I, who went forth this morning so heart-broken and depressed!" And the tears sprang into his bright eyes in spite of himself.

"What was your first thought, Joseph, when he opened your eyes today?" asked Marcus.

Joseph stopped his excited walking and sat down soberly enough, facing Marcus. A wonderful look of reverence and love stole over his face as he said softly:

"The first thing I saw when my eyes were opened was the face of Jesus bending over me, and my first thought was, 'Thou are the Christ, the Holy One of God!'"

Everything was silence for some moments, then Marcus said:

"Believest thou he is the promised Messiah?"

"With my whole heart," said the youth; and Aunt Eunice whispered "Amen."

"Joseph," said Marcus, presently. "I started out to find a messenger for my uncle's palace, this morning. God seems to have led me here. Wilt thou take the place?"

"Dost think I could worthily fill it?" asked Joseph, earnestly.

"Thy very question is sufficient answer in itself," said Marcus. "He whose first thought is to honor the place he fills, instead of scheming to have the place honor him, is sure to fill it worthily. If thou art willing to go, I shall be glad to take thee," he added, rising.

"I will do my best," was Joseph's answer; and they went away together, after bidding adieu to Ruth and her aunt.

Joseph was soon uniformed and installed in his new office, where he became one of the most trusted messengers.

9

Leave God to order all thy ways,
And hope in him, whate'er betide.
Thou'lt find him, in the evil days,
Thy all-sufficient strength and guide.
Who trusts in God's unchanging love
Builds on the Rock that naught can move.

~ George Neumarck.

"Marcus," said Miriam, a few days after the events narrated in the last chapter, "I like the face of Joseph, thy new messenger. It is an honest, true face. I long to hear him tell of how Jesus healed him of his blindness. I want also to hear his little sister tell the story; they say she is very bright and pretty, and that it was through her faith and prayers that Jesus healed both Joseph and herself. Could she not come to us in my mother's rooms, and could not Joseph also come there with thee?"

"If my honored aunt, thy mother, will it so, I will be more than glad to bring them there at any time," said Marcus.

"She not only is willing, but anxious, to see and hear them both, and my father also desires to know when they come, that he too, may hear the story from their own lips.

"At what hour shall I bring them?"

"Oh, Marcus, soon! I am so impatient to hear them that I cannot wait."

"An hour hence, then, let it be. I saw it all, and it was wonderful, indeed! I am more than anxious that thou shouldest hear the story from their own lips."

"Thou didst see it all! Would that I, too, could see this wondrous man! Tell me again, my Marcus, how Ruth sprang upon her crippled feet without a thought. Oh, it was wonderful!"

"She had wholly forgotten herself in thinking of her brother. Indeed, she had asked nothing for herself, but only that his sight might be restored. And when Jesus leaned over him and looked on his sightless eyes, her gaze was riveted upon her brother's face, feeling, as she now says, that there was not a doubt that he would be healed. When she saw the long-sealed lids unclose, and Joseph look up into the face of Jesus, she gave one rapturous cry and sprang lightly upon her feet, without a thought of their helplessness, and fell upon her brother's neck for joy. Her 'faith had changed to sight, her hope to fruition.'"

"And what did Joseph do? Tell me again."

"Gathered her to his heart and cried, 'Thou, too, my little sister, thou, too, art healed!'"

"And then she knew!" said Miriam, with dilated, tear-filled eyes.

"Yes, then she knew that God had doubly honored her faith," said Marcus. "But now, my Miriam, thou must rest, thy nerves are all unstrung; and an hour hence I will bring Joseph and Ruth to thy honored mother's room."

"It fills me with such peace to hear these things," said Miriam, as she turned and joined Ayeah, waiting at a little distance for her, and reentered the palace. An hour later, they all were gathered in the salon in the mother's wing of the palace, when Marcus entered with Joseph and his sister. The manners of both were modest and attractive, without subservience, when they were presented to Jairus and his wife, and Ruth's face grew very bright when she looked on Miriam. They told their wonderful story simply and without embellishment, and answered all questions asked by Jairus and his wife with unaffected simplicity, though both faces shone with an almost divine light, as they spoke of Jesus.

"Dost thou then believe, Joseph," said Jairus, "that this Jesus of Nazareth, who truly hath wonderfully restored thy sight and put new life into the paralyzed limbs of thy little sister, is the promised Christ?"

"How else could he do these things?" said Joseph, respectfully. "Yes, my master, I do believe he is the promised Christ, so often foretold by the prophets."

Jairus made no reply, but he held out his hand to his daughter sitting close beside him and drew her to his heart. Her tears had flown freely during the narrative, and now she whispered to her father:

"May I not have Ruth as my companion? She is so bright and lovely! I am sure she would make me happy."

Jairus looked at the golden-haired girl with face like a meadow lily, with a beauty from which even the plain garb of her class could not detract, and his heart warmed instinctively to her. But he only said softly to Miriam:

"Art thou not then happy, my little daughter?"

"Oh, very, very happy, my father; but at times I am lonely, when not with thee or my mother or Marcus. Then Ruth would be a comfort. I could teach her to embroider and to read to me, and she could do many little things that Ayeah is too old to learn."

The father listened, smoothing her soft hair, and all the time scrutinizingly observing the stranger maiden. At length he held his hand out to Ruth, and when she Came to him, he said: "Wouldest thou like to be always near my daughter Miriam?"

"Oh," said Ruth, delightedly, "could I wait on her, and braid her hair, and fan her while she slept, and—"

"Yes," said Miriam's father, smiling, "I suppose it would be something like that, would it not, Miriam?"

Miriam was now sitting up beside her father, and she drew Ruth to her, putting her arm around her and saying wistfully:

"And wouldest thou love me, little Ruth?"

"That I already do," and, bending over Miriam, she tenderly kissed the fragile hand of the girl.

"Well, go and talk it over with thy mother. I see no reason why it should not be, if it will make thee happy."

Miriam's mother sent for Ruth's Aunt Eunice, and soon the matter was settled that Ruth should be adopted into the household of Jairus, as well as her brother. And not only did this happy lot fall to Ruth and Joseph, but the wife of Jairus, with true womanly delicacy, said to their Aunt Eunice:

"Since we have taken your son and daughter from you, you must permit us also to adopt you, in a measure, and supply in part what otherwise they would have done for you." And thenceforth, from the great house went a constant supply of the necessaries of life to the widow's cottage, so that the last years of her life were full of rest and peace.

"Joseph," she said to her nephew, on one of his visits to her, "God's ravens have indeed brought to us a bountiful supply; we did well to trust him!"

"Indeed, yes, aunt!" was Joseph's glad reply. "And your faith never failed, even when mine was weakest, in those our darkest days."

"Ruth was often my monitor," said her aunt. "She is an angel of blessing in our house," said Joseph. "I do not wonder that Jesus loved and listened to her, when she pleaded for me. Oh, Aunt Eunice! what would my life have been but for his mercy that day? And now we are all watching to find him when he is here and ask him to heal our mistress, Miriam. She is patient and lovely, and such a sufferer! And we feel that Jesus would heal all of her infirmities. She believes in him fully. She says Ruth is such a comfort and blessing to her, and she never wearies of having Ruth talk to her about the day he met us at the gate."

10

She is not dead, but sleepeth.—Luke 8: 52.

Be patient, suffering soul! I hear thy cry.
The trial fires may glow, but I am nigh.
I see the silver, and I will refine
Until my image shall upon it shine.
Fear not, for I am near, thy help to be;
Greater than all thy pain, my love for thee.

~ H.C.W.

A few days after this visit of Joseph to his aunt, and some little time after he had entered into the service of Jairus, Ruth was in Miriam's private room, engaged in the, to her, delightful employment of brushing out the long, beautiful hair of her young mistress. Suddenly Miriam threw up her arms, and with a stifled cry, fell forward from the couch upon which she was sitting to the floor, in violent convulsions. Ayeah, who was never far distant from her, rushed forward, and lifting her into her arms, laid her tenderly upon the couch and began chafing the bloodless hands, calling to Ruth to run quickly for Miriam's mother and the palace physician.

Ruth never had seen Miriam so violently ill before, and was greatly alarmed. She hastened to do as she was bidden, and soon the frightened household were gathered about the bed of the beloved sufferer.

"Oh! may not Joseph seek for Jesus?" Ruth exclaimed, with trembling lips, as Miriam's mother fell, half fainting, beside the couch on which her daughter lay, evidently dying.

Miriam's dull ear caught the name and her pale lips gasped, "Jesus!"

"Go! go!" said Jairus to Marcus. "Seek thou for the prophet till he is found. Let Joseph also go, and if you find him, quickly bring me word."

The two young men ran hurriedly out in different directions, if haply they might find him on whom alone their hopes now hung. Meanwhile, convulsion after convulsion shook the form of the sufferer, each one leaving her weaker and with less hope of recovery. There would come, now and then, a lucid interval, when she would look pleadingly into the agonized faces of her father and mother as they bent over her, and whisper, "Jesus." In one of these, the father whispered to her:

"Marcus hath gone to seek him; Joseph hath also gone; they soon will come."

"Go thou likewise," she murmured. Then the dread paroxysm came.

"Yes. go!" the frantic mother pleaded; "thou mayest find him, and thy presence here cannot save her."

So the agonized father himself went hurriedly forth. In the outer court he met Joseph, breathless from haste.

"He is at the house of Matthew, the publican. There has been a great feast; it is now over, but they are still at table. Thou wilt find him there."

"Thank God that he is found! Tell thy mistress that he is found, and bid her tell Miriam when she next rouses that he will soon be here." But alas! there were to come no more lucid intervals to the poor sufferer; for even as the father was talking, the guileless spirit had slipped from its tenement of clay. Not knowing this, the father hastened with all speed to the house of Matthew, where he indeed found Jesus still sitting by the table talking to those about him, although the feast itself was ended. Jairus threw himself at the feet of Jesus, crying:

"Master, my little daughter, my only and well-beloved child, is dying. If thou wilt but come and lay thy hand upon her she will live. To thee alone the power of saving her is given." The father's agony and his evident faith in Jesus touched with compassion the heart of the teacher, and he arose at once and signified his willingness to accompany him. As they pressed their way through the crowd outside, that had grown very great, Jesus suddenly turned and asked, "Who touched me?" Simon Peter, the practical, said to him, "The multitude presseth thee on every side, and askest thou, 'Who touched me?'" But Jesus knew someone with faith in his power to heal had touched him, to be rid of some disease. And, as he turned about and looked, a woman cast herself, weeping, at his feet, confessing that she had but "touched the hem of his garment," and that she was instantly healed of an infirmity from which for twelve years she had suffered. Did Jesus rebuke her? Nay, he only said kindly, "Daughter, go in peace; thy faith hath saved thee." And from that hour she was well.

Jesus laid his hand in blessing on her head.

All of this, together with the great crowd through which they had to pass, delayed Jesus and Jairus, so that, long before they could reach the palace gates, Joseph met them and said to Jairus:

"They sent me to tell thee that our little mistress Miriam is already dead, and thou needest not trouble the prophet. But oh, my master!" Joseph added, softly, "he hath power even to raise the dead!"

Jesus heard the words, and turning a kindly look upon the young man, said gently to Jairus, "Fear not; only believe," and the words and look put fresh courage into the father's heart as they pressed on.

Reaching the palace, they found the house filled with hired mourners, and the little maid already prepared for burial, while the stricken mother was wailing beside the bier, and Marcus and Ruth were standing motionless behind the draperies of the great window. Seeing Ayeah near the doorway, crouching down in her sorrow, Jesus touched her gently upon the shoulder, and when she looked up, said:

"Prepare nourishing food and bring it at once to the room of thy little mistress, that she may eat!"

With startled eyes she looked up into his face and wailed:

"My Master, she will never eat again. The maid is dead."

"Nay, she but sleepeth," he answered her.

The hired mourners laughed scornfully at him, but he put them all out of the room and bade Joseph keep watch beside the door, admitting none.

Then he took Peter, James and John into the room where Jairus and his wife were alone with their dead child, and approaching the couch whereon the still form rested, he took the pale hands into one of his own, and with the other hand touched the waxen eyelids, saying gently:

"Maiden, arise!"

The white lids slowly opened, and the dark eyes for an instant looked wonderingly up into the face above her; then a smile broke over her face, and she said softly:

"I have waited long, but I knew that thou wouldest come."

Jesus smiled back into the dreamy eyes, and lifting her to her feet, laid his hands in blessing on her head, then bade them feed her with the food Ayeah had prepared.

The crowd outside was quietly dispersed by Jairus himself appearing and telling them the young girl was well and quietly eating the food prepared for her. Miriam took the food as Ayeah gave it to her, but when Jesus would have quietly passed from the room, she arose and stretched forth her hands appealingly to him, crying:

"Jesus! Teacher! Leave me not, I entreat thee!"

He turned and passed swiftly to her side again, his face full of tenderness, and taking her hands in his, bent over her and whispered softly:

"Thou art indeed one of my very own, my child. I shall often see thee: I will never be far away from thee. Canst trust me?"

Miriam had been covering his hands with her tears and kisses, and now she raised her tearful face, radiant with smiles, and said joyously:

"Oh, if thou wilt surely return to me, wilt sometimes take up thine abode with us, I will be content."

"I will return," he said. "Never fear; I will return before many days." And, once more laying his hands upon her head in blessing, he passed through the room into the corridor without. There, by the entrance where he had placed Joseph on guard, he found him still standing, and by him his sister Ruth.

"Thou art a faithful guard," Jesus said, smiling kindly upon the young lad, and added, "Thou art now free to go to thy other duties; be faithful in all things as thou hast been in this, if thou wouldest conquer."

Then Joseph and Ruth fell on their knees before him, crying.

"Blessed teacher, dost thou not know us?" Joseph said. "Thou didst heal us at the great gates. We have sought thee everywhere."

"Yes, I know you both. You are such as my Father loves."

"Thou art the Christ. Thou art the promised Messiah," said Ruth, reverently, lifting her sweet child face to his, radiant with love.

Miriam was very quiet, saying little throughout the day, but her face was radiant with a joy and peace. Marcus hovered about her with delight and awe upon his face, and her father and mother never left her room, though they refrained from talking much with her. Something holy seemed to have dropped about her as a mantle, and all recognized and paid it honor. Ruth sat on a footstool at her feet, scarcely removing her eyes from the happy face, and her own face was scarcely less radiant, while Ayeah crouched on the floor in a corner of the room and still looked dazed, bewildered and happy.

What an event had happened to that entire household that day! Into each heart, from that of Jairus down to the humble slave woman, had come the certainty that Christ, the Son of God, had entered into their dwelling and called back to life their beloved one; and their hearts were overcome with awe and gratitude. What had happened to Miriam in that brief space of unconsciousness? "Did she herself know?" wondered each heart. At last, toward evening, Miriam said dreamily:

"Marcus, was I asleep when Jesus came today?"

"Yes, dear," he replied, quietly.

"In a perfectly dead sleep, was I not?"

"I think so; why do you ask?"

"I think I must have been dreaming at the time," she said. "I thought I was walking in a wondrously beautiful garden, full of trees and fountains and flowers and birds, and little children everywhere. A lovely bright being walked beside me, but somehow, I felt that for some reason I shrank from him and wanted to go over and join the children. And then I looked up and saw coming directly towards us the very man that I had dreamed of when a child. As he approached us he held out his hand, so that the angel with me stopped.

"Then Jesus said (for now I know it is he), 'There is still much for her to do,' and, taking my hand, he turned me about, and together we walked back the way I had come, the angel passing on and leaving us alone together. We walked on a little way in silence, then, as we were passing a fragrant bank of flowers, I said, 'Teacher, I am very tired; may I rest?'

'Assuredly you may,' he answered gently; 'rest on these fragrant blossoms,' leading me into their midst. I lay down, and I think I must have fallen asleep at once, for the next I knew I heard his voice saying, 'Maid, arise.' And I was surprised to find I was here in my own room, and Jesus was bending over me."

"But you spoke at once to him, as though you were expecting him," said Marcus.

"Yes, I was not at all surprised to see him here."

Hearing her talking, her parents came forward to where she was sitting, and Jairus said tenderly:

"How is my daughter now?"

"Well, my father, well—and oh, so happy! Is it not almost too wonderful to believe that the Christ has been to us within our very doors, and has brought strength and health to me? To me!"

She raised her bright face to her mother, and reaching up her arms, drew her face down against her own, whispering, "My mother! My beloved mother!"

The mother drew her to her heart, and the long-suppressed excitement broke forth in sobs, as she said, brokenly:

"Oh, my precious daughter, it would indeed have been a desolate house this evening, if he had not come!"

Miriam drew her head back, so that she could look her mother in the face, and said in a half-startled way:

"Mother! Was I then already dead?"

Everyone was startled at the question, and no one answered. She looked from one to the other in turn, then seeing Ruth at her feet, she leaned forward and placed her hand under Ruth's chin, turned the child-face up till the eyes met her own, and looking straight into their depths, she slowly questioned:

"Ruth, thou never didst deceive me; tell me truly: Was I dead?"

The great tear-drops rolled down Ruth's cheeks, but she could not speak.

"I am answered," said Miriam, kissing Ruth's forehead as she spoke. "Then I was not dreaming, but really walking in spirit with the Christ. And that must have been the angel of death with whom I walked at first. Well, he was beautiful; but I shrank from him—perhaps because it was not God's will that he should take me yet. Is it not passing strange? I have been out of the body, yet am still here. Oh, my father! my mother!"—giving a hand to each —"shall we not follow the teachings of this wonderful Christ? Shall we not be a household,"—looking around upon them all—"of his devoted followers?"

The tears were in all eyes as Jairus, bending over, kissed his little daughter and whispered brokenly, "We will."

"And he will come and teach us. He promised he would come," she continued, eagerly.

"Yes, dearest, he will come. But now if we are to keep our daughter well as he has made her, we must do our part, and not allow her to exhaust her strength. Ayeah will bring your evening meal, then help you retire for the night. And may the blessed Christ send you refreshing slumber," said her mother.

"Oh, my mother, I am so strong and well! Must I really go so early?"

"It is best, my daughter."

"Then I will do whatever thou shalt bid me. I am my mother's daughter, as well as a disciple of Jesus of Nazareth. My love for him intensifies my love and reverence for thee."

11

I've found a friend; oh, such a friend!
He loved me ere I knew Him;
He drew me with the cords of love,
And thus He bound me to Him.
And 'round my heart still closely twine
Those ties which naught can sever;
For I am His, and He is mine,
Forever and forever.

~ J. G. SMALL.

"I wonder," said Miriam, a few days after her wonderful restoration, "I wonder why Jesus does not come to us? He promised that he would."

She was standing at a window in the palace and was looking wistfully down the narrow street. Even the few days had wrought a great change in the young girl. The sickly pallor, so often, heretofore, on her face, was entirely gone, and the flesh looked roseate and full of life. The large eyes were no longer languid, but full of a clear, happy light; the hitherto feeble step had grown firm and elastic; and she flew from room to room and from corridor to garden, singing with the freedom and abandon of a bird. It was almost impossible to believe she was the same maiden so long the anxiety and care of her father's household. Ayeah had lost her lifelong charge, and seemed bewildered, as though she could not comprehend the change. Ruth glowed with happiness, and flitted here and there with a buoyancy unusual even to her, and many and inexhaustible were the conversations she and Miriam held about the great teacher. It was to her Miriam had addressed her remark in the opening of the chapter.

"We must not forget, my mistress, that we are not the only ones who need his help, and long for the presence of Jesus," Ruth softly said. "To both of us he hath already given wonderful strength and health, and I am sure it is but natural and right that we should wish to be near him, but—there are others who need him more. Forgive me, dear Miriam, but what would Joseph and poor I have done but for his blessed habit of 'going about doing good'?"

"You are right, my Ruth; and we must not be selfish, much as our hearts yearn for him. He will come very soon, however, I am sure, because you know he promised that he would."

"Yes, he will come soon; in that you are right, I know. He will come soon, because he knows we love him," said Ruth, with sparkling eyes.

"Come, let us go into the garden for our morning walk, while the dew yet hangs upon the leaf," said Miriam, stretching forth her hand to Ruth; and the two girls ran joyously through the corridors, down the great marble stairway, and on out into the garden with its fragrant shrubs and flowers. They visited the sundial, but it was still too early for the shadow to be cast, strolled through the beautiful walks, gathered the dew-laden flowers, and finally, went to the arbor to rest awhile in its inviting shadows. At the entrance to the arbor, both girls stopped in amazement, for there, quietly seated near the table, they saw Jesus, with a happy smile of greeting for them upon his face.

"Teacher!" they cried simultaneously, throwing themselves upon their knees beside him and pressing his hands to their lips in loving reverence.

"Peace be unto you, dear maidens," he said gently. Then seating himself beside them, he conversed of the many things their hearts were longing to know. Ayeah, who as usual watched near Miriam, hurried to her mistress and told her the welcome news that Jesus was talking with the children in the garden, and soon both she and her husband Jairus hastened to welcome him and do him honor.

They constrained him to enter the palace and partake with them of the morning meal; and the food that with uplifted hands he blessed was sweeter than any of which they had ever partaken before. As they sat at table, he unfolded to them the word of life and wrapped them about with his wonderful and exalted love.

When at last he raised his hands above them in blessing and rose to depart, Jairus said fervently, "Teacher, thou hast truly given to us the words of eternal life, and from this time forth, I and my household will worship the Father at thy feet."

From that time, he often came to spend an hour in their midst, and sometimes rested for a night beneath their roof; and the entire atmosphere of the palace became one of unmixed joy and peace.

12

*So love in our hearts shall grow mighty and strong,
Through crosses, through sorrows, through manifold wrong.*

~ H. W. Longfellow.

So wonderful was the change wrought in Miriam, both physically and spiritually, that her life began to unfold like the flower-buds—too long deprived of the sun—when brought into its life-giving light. From being a delicate, oversensitive child, in a few months she had developed into a strong, healthy, active young woman, full of life and energy, and endowed with rare intellectual and spiritual graces. Not only had her wonderful healing brought about this change from the first, but the constant intercourse with Jesus, as he came and went in her father's household, kept her spirit fed with that life-giving food that alone can make us both physically and spiritually whole. One interview with the blessed Christ, however satisfying it may be at the time, is not enough to make us grow into the strong, beautiful characters it is his wish we should become; but we must drink daily from the fountain of life, a draught that can be taken only from his hands.

As the months passed and the great change in Miriam's life became apparent to all, Marcus pleaded that their long betrothal might now terminate in marriage; and to this both Jairus and his wife gave ready consent, for Marcus was already as a son to them, and they were quite ready to trust their darling to his care, especially so since it would not remove her from their household. So it came to pass that, before the year had closed, she became the wife of Marcus. And Jesus was at the wedding feast, and before he left, he laid his hands in blessing upon the heads of the young couple whose lives were henceforth to be as one, and spoke to them words of tender counsel and advice.

So the two happy young lives rounded out in symmetry and beauty; their intercourse with Jesus, the example of his beautiful life and the purity and exalted character of his teaching lifted them on to a higher plane of existence than they had ever reached before. They became his most earnest and devoted followers, and no pleasure was so great to them as to frequent the synagogue where he regularly taught when in Capernaum. One day, a short time after their marriage, Marcus came home with a troubled look upon his face, unusual to him.

"What is it, Marcus?" said Miriam, always quick to notice any change in his demeanor, as he threw himself into a seat beside her. "What troubles thee, my Marcus?"

"How quick thou art, Miriam, to see any shadow on my face!" said Marcus, tenderly.

"How could it be otherwise," asked she, "when thou art now my greatest study? Thy face is now my book; in it I read all that I seek to know," she answered brightly. "But tell me now, in truth, what troubles thee."

"Yes, I will tell thee, Miriam, for thy heart is as devoted to the Nazarene as my own."

"Has evil then befallen Jesus?" asked Miriam, with startled eyes.

"No actual evil yet, though I fear it threatens him. I saw Aurelius—he whom I met some time ago with Antonius at the bath—in the synagogue this morning as Jesus taught. With him were three other men, with sinister faces and evil eyes. They kept their heads together and whispered and watched Jesus, and sneered covertly at all that he said. When they left the synagogue, I learned that they sought the other rulers; thy father they did not undertake to see again, for his position toward Jesus is well known. They are spies, I doubt not, sent hither from Jerusalem to trap him into saying something they can use against him."

"But, Marcus, all he saith is so pure and good. Why should they want to misrepresent him? They cannot injure him; he hath done so much good, the people would all rise up and defend him."

"The people are not always grateful, Miriam. Dost thou remember, when last year we all went to Jerusalem with thy honored father and mother to visit my father, how thy tender heart ached for that wretched cripple who seemed always to be watching for the 'troubling of the water' in the great pool by the sheep-gate?"

"The one that told us that for thirty-eight years he had been so crippled by paralysis that he was unable to move at all without assistance?"

"The same. Well, Jesus one day noticed his wretchedness, and his compassionate heart was touched by the dreadful infirmity of the man, and he said to him, 'Wouldest thou be made whole?' Then it seems the man told him how long he had been ill, and how he was daily brought to the Pool of Bethesda to seek healing in its waters, but being helpless, was unable to get into the water, as he had no man near to help him. Then Jesus said to him, 'Arise, take up thy bed, and walk!' And taking him by the hand, he lifted him to his feet, which immediately received strength; and he, taking up his bed, started homeward to tell the glad news to others. Jesus, in the meantime, disappeared in the crowd always collected about the pool; and the crippled man, never having seen Jesus until that day, knew not who had healed him. This had all happened upon the Sabbath day, and thou knowest it is forbidden in the letter of the law for anyone to bear a burden upon that day; but in this case it surely was admissible that the man should carry his bed to his home, as it probably was the only one he had, and he could not afford to lose it by leaving it beside the pool. It does not seem to me that his act could be construed into a breach of the law, as it was not burden bearing in the common acceptation of the term. But some of the caviling Jews thought otherwise, and taxed him with breaking the law.

"'I do not wish to break the law,' he answered them, 'but he who made me whole bade me take up my bed and walk.'

"'And who was he?' they questioned.

"'I know not,' he said.! I only know that paralyzed for thirty-eight years, he healed me by his touch; but who he was I know not.'

"'He has caused thee to violate the law,' they said threateningly; for they knew that no one but Jesus could have done this miracle, and they wanted to gather proof against him. A few days later Jesus again met the man, restored and well, in the temple. Jesus must have known that he had used this new God-given strength in a sinful manner, for he spoke a word of warning to him:

"'Thou hast been made whole; sin no more, lest a worse thing come upon thee.' Then the man knew it was Jesus that had healed him. What did he do? Fall down and worship him? Nay! He went and told the Jews that it was Jesus who healed him! To free himself from the charge of breaking the law, he accused this man—who had given back to him life and strength—of the sin of enticing him to do wrong. What think you of such gratitude?"

A bright red spot burned in each of Miriam's cheeks, and she said hotly:

"May he be overtaken in his sin and pay its heaviest penalty! How could he be so base? How could he fail to recognize the Christ?"

"All do not see with thy clear vision, my Miriam. This poor man was evidently all 'of the earth, earthy.' He had no inner vision of the spiritual beauty of Jesus, as you have, my wife. He was healed, and that being the sum, the acme of his desires, he had no care for anything else. It mattered nothing to him who suffered because of his supposed sin, so he himself escaped unpunished."

"I cannot understand how anyone could feel thus. I knew that I was healed, when Jesus gave me back my life—I felt it in every fiber of my being—but, over and above the gratitude the gift engendered, there sprang into life, in the very depths of my heart, a love which I had never known before. It took possession of me, it filled my life. I cannot describe it to thee, Marcus, but it was as deep as the ocean and as high as heaven itself. The healing, though I was conscious of it, was secondary to me. I could only think of him. He filled every want of my life, and so engrossed my thoughts, especially for the first hours, that I wanted to be silent, that I might think of him."

"I remember how silent and absorbed thou wast—for hours after Jesus left—that memorable day," said Marcus, tenderly stroking the hand he held.

"I could not talk, he so filled my heart. Canst thou understand it, Marcus?" she asked, a little wistfully.

"I do understand it most thoroughly, my wife," he answered. "I love him with a love scarcely less than thine own. He is seldom absent from my thoughts. Nothing human could call forth such depth and tenderness of feeling. His restoring thee to life and giving thee back to us when we thought we had lost thee here forever, would naturally call for our deepest love and gratitude; but, Miriam, my precious wife, I loved him long before he had laid this claim upon us," said Marcus, with deep feeling. A silence fell upon them that seemed almost holy, and each seemed absorbed in happy thought. "If," Marcus at length resumed, "he were but a mortal man, we would say it was the result of his exalted character. We would speak of his unselfish life, so given to thought for others; of his filial love, of his loyalty to his friends, of his tenderness for little children and his reverence for the aged, of his purity in every thought, word and act of his life; for these all go to make up a character beyond compare. But it is something beyond this that calls forth from us the depth of tenderness and reverence and love: that compels us, were it necessary, even to lay down our lives for his sake."

"Oh, Marcus!" said Miriam, almost tearfully, "and that makes us love each other better, because of our great love for him!"

"Yes," said Marcus, "that makes us partakers of the divinity within himself, and"— after a moment's pause—"that compels me now to leave the company dearer to me than any on earth, that if possible, I may warn him of the danger I fear threatens him, and seek to aid him in escaping it."

"Oh, go at once!" said Miriam, eagerly, "and, if possible, induce him to return hither with thee. Tell him the guest chamber, now peculiarly his own, is always ready for him, and that we wait with eager hearts his coming."

13

I know for me the thread of life is slender,
And soon with me the labor will be wrought;
Then grows my heart to other hearts more tender.
The time is short.

~ Dinah Craik.

The day was closing, and the cool breezes of the evening were ruffling the blue waters of the sea, before Marcus—for whom Miriam had anxiously watched for hours —returned; and with him came Jesus. A great peace fell upon Miriam's heart when she heard their steps in the corridor and knew that Jesus had accompanied her husband on his return, and would spend the night beneath their roof.

A great anxiety had taken hold of her, since her talk with her husband earlier in the day, about Jesus. She felt that a great danger menaced him, and her heart rebelled at the thought that one so pure and good in every way should be persecuted thus by evil men. The fact that it was the priests who instigated this persecution only made her the more rebellious, since she felt that they, of all men, should sustain and befriend him. Now that she knew he was safely beneath their roof, and that she would soon see the face she so loved, and listen to the voice that sent new life to her heart, she was content and glad, and waited patiently till he should come to her. Marcus had taken him direct to the guest chamber, where a slave awaited to administer the refreshing bath and anoint the weary feet. When, refreshed and invigorated, he came with her husband into the room, her heart was so full of joy at beholding him, she could only advance to meet him with outstretched hands, saying gently:

"I am so glad to see thee again. A thousand welcomes to our home."

But her radiant face and tender eyes told of the royal welcome her heart accorded him, and his voice was more than usually gentle as he answered:

"It is always a joy to me to form one of thy household, my daughter, whenever it is permitted me to do so." And he held her outstretched hands closely in his own.

Jairus and his wife entered the room at this moment and also gave him a hearty welcome. Soon thereafter the evening repast was served, and afterward they all ascended to the housetop and sat beneath the stars.

Who can tell of the blessedness of those hours when they crowded close about him and listened to the words from his sacred lips? The soft starlight fell about them, and in the garden beneath a nightingale sang softly, as though it would not disturb the sacredness of the hour. Before ascending to the roof, Jairus, at the wish of Jesus, had assembled all the servants together in the outer court, and Jesus had talked a little with them in simple, loving language, and blessed them all, for he had ever a message for the lowliest. And now he sat with the household alone, in the sacredness of the night hour upon the housetop, overlooking the Sea of Galilee, and the beauty of the stars above them was reflected in the tranquil waters of the sea beneath them. Miriam sat close at his left hand, Marcus was upon his right, while Jairus and his wife sat facing him; and Ruth, whom Miriam had thoughtfully called, crouched at his feet, the unspoken rapture of her heart shining through her face. Joseph, too, sat a little apart from Marcus, but near enough to hear all that was said. His face, too, showed how sincere the love and homage of his heart for Jesus.

Jesus talked to them of his Father's wondrous love and mercy, of the life beyond, to which that of earth is but the prelude, of the "house of many mansions," and the glories and happiness of the eternal city. Their hearts grew more and more tender as he talked with them, and turned to him with a deeper love than ever before. He told them of the long journey he was soon to take, going from city to city to proclaim the gospel of the Son of God, reaching at last Jerusalem, where his ministry was to end. They well understood that he spoke of his life as well as his work being ended there, and their hearts were filled with sorrow. Few words were spoken for hours by anyone but Jesus, though now and then a question would be asked. Once, Miriam, slipping her fingers within his own, whispered brokenly, "Why this long absence, my teacher? How can we do without thy teaching and thy love? May we not hope that thou will soon return to us?"

His fingers closely pressed her own as he answered:

"What I have already taught thee, thou wilt not forget, and my love will abide with thee forever. I shall probably return hither for a few hours before going up to Jerusalem, but not for many days—the time is short. But I shall see thee in Jerusalem, in thy father's house," he said, turning to Marcus. "He, together with Nicodemus and many others, has long served me in secret. Open espousal of my cause would only expose them to persecution and prevent their doing for me the many kind services it is their evident delight to do."

"I know," said Marcus, sadly. "The last time I saw my honored father he said to me very earnestly, 'John Mark (my baptismal name, and the one by which my father always calls me), if it be necessary, die to save that good man from the hatred of these evil men, who would even sacrifice his life for their wicked purposes.'"

"It would do no good, my son," said Jesus, "though from my heart I thank thee. Only my life will satisfy them. John Mark is a good name. By it thou shall be called, and by it known through countless generations."

"But why," Jairus said earnestly, "Why go to Jerusalem at all? Why subject thyself to the power of these evil men? In that city their power is unbounded. Why not remain with those who love and trust thee, knowing thee as thou art—the Son of God?"

"My Father wills it otherwise. It is expedient for you that I go away, but my peace will remain with you forever. These men who seek my life do not believe that I am sent forth from the Father, but if I be lifted up, I shall draw all men unto me, and through me to the Father."

These words were sorrowfully spoken, and each heart felt, foretold not only his death, but the manner of his death. Every heart was filled with sorrow. Ruth laid her face upon the sandaled feet of the teacher she so loved and bathed them with her tears. Miriam leaned her head against his arm, and her mother's face was wet with tears. A solemn silence was over all. Jairus and Marcus each sat with stern, sad faces, and Joseph hid his bowed face in his hands, to conceal his not unmanly tears.

Then Jesus, visibly moved by their great love for him, again spoke, and his voice was full of a strange, deep tenderness. He passed his arm about Miriam's trembling form and drew her more closely to his side, and placed his right hand caressingly upon the bowed head of Ruth, as he said:

"'Let not your hearts be troubled.' Ye all believe and trust in the Father's boundless love and mercy; believe also the words I speak unto you, when I say that all he wills that I should do and suffer, I gladly;— nay, joyfully— do and bear, that his name may be glorified before the world. It was for this that I came into the world: shall I not fulfill the will of him who sent me? Were I to ask, he would send legions of angels to deliver me; but then would the purpose for which I came be unfulfilled. Be strong, beloved friends, and by your courage and love assist me to meet the trial awaiting me."

Then he, too, bowed his head and sat in silent thought. Peter quietly joined the group at this time, and was silently recognized by Jesus and Jairus with a kindly glance. He sat down near Marcus, of whom he was very fond, and whom he also called John Mark, having known him from his childhood. It was Peter who had first spoken to him of the wonderful prophet of Nazareth, and had led him to believe on him as the Son of the Most High. Hence the bond between the two had become very marked and strong, and many believe that it was through Peter's influence that the "Gospel of Mark" was afterward written by Marcus —or John Mark—wherein the life, suffering and death of the Savior of mankind are so vividly and faithfully portrayed.

Long they sat in silent, thoughtful communion. Then Jesus, rising, said:

"Let us sing our morning hymn before we part." And, Jesus leading with a voice attuned like a heavenly harp, they sang together the sublime words of King David:

> Praise ye the Lord.
> Praise ye the Lord from the heavens;
> Praise him in the heights.
> Praise ye him, all his angels;
> Praise ye him, all his hosts!
> Praise ye him, sun and moon;
> Praise him, all ye stars of light.
> Praise him, ye heaven of heavens,
> And ye waters that be above the heavens.
> Kings of the earth, and all people;
> Princes and all judges of the earth;

Both young men and maidens;
Old men and children;
Let them praise the name of the Lord;
For his name alone is excellent:
His glory is above the earth and heaven.
Let everything that hath breath praise the Lord.
Praise ye the Lord.

The song ceased, and raising his hands above them, he breathed a short prayer, full of tenderness and pathos, petitioning the Father to keep these, so beloved by him, from all evil, and preserve them blameless in his sight. He prayed that they might be led by the Holy Spirit in the way of all truth, and that the Comforter might take up his abode with them, and more than fill the vacancy, more than soothe the pain their coming separation from him would produce. Then he blessed them fervently, and descended to the room provided for him. Marcus accompanied him to the door of his chamber, then he and all the others retired to their respective rooms for a few hours' rest. The stars were paling in the heavens, and the first gray shadows of the dawn were stealing over the hilltops. They had watched through the night together, and the memory of that marvelous vigil would remain in every heart forever.

Miriam lay down upon her couch, but she could not rest. The events of the night had taken such hold of her sensitive mind, that they drove sleep from her pillow. At length she arose, and throwing a heavy robe about her to protect her from the chill air, she once again ascended to the roof. The fleecy clouds that lay banked up in the east, when she had descended to her room, were now a mass of purple and rose, with golden rays shooting athwart them, and their ragged edges tipped with burnished gold. She heard a step, and turning, saw her husband close beside her. She gave him a look of grateful welcome and slipped her hand into his own as he approached her, but no word was spoken by either; in silence they looked upon the grandeur of the scene. Mt. Hermon, in the far distance to the north, wore a crown of light upon his snow-capped head; the Mount of the Beatitudes, only a few miles away toward the southwest, blushed with pleasure, as the sunlight chased the shadows down its rugged sides. The Sea of Galilee was like a lake of fire in its rosy glory, that gradually changed into a sea of molten gold as the wavelets, gold-tipped, chased each other in rapid succession across its breast. Marcus and Miriam stood entranced by the beautiful sight.

Marcus and Miriam

It stood a gigantic cross.

Suddenly, as they looked, out of its golden depths in the center of the lake, a pillar of silver light slowly arose, mounting upward, upward to the height of perhaps one hundred feet. At first, they thought it the vapor that so often rested on the lake at dawn, but the breeze that drifted across its bosom did not disturb it, or cause it even to vacillate. Then, from either side of the column, an arm reached out, and now it stood a gigantic cross of silver rising from its base of gold. A moment it stood immovable, then, slowly parting from its foundation, it rose upward until it was distinctly outlined against the clouds of purple and rose, when it gradually faded away and was lost amid the broken, floating clouds. Each young heart drew a heavy breath, when, as they looked downward, Marcus and Miriam saw Jesus standing upon the shore, looking over the sea. He had gone out in the early dawn, as was his usual custom, to walk beside the waters he so loved. Turning and looking upward he saw the two standing upon the roof, and with a gentle smile, waved his hand to them, and walking swiftly onward, was soon lost to view. Had he, too, seen the cross?

14

> O Master, it is good to be
> Entranced, enwrapt, alone with Thee;
> And watch Thy glistening raiment glow
> Whiter than Hermon's whitest snow;
> The human lineaments that shine
> Irradiant with a light divine;
> Till we, too, change from grace to grace,
> Gazing on that transfigured face.
>
> ~ Arthur P. Stanley.

The night after the events narrated in the preceding chapter, Marcus was sleepless and restless, and rising in the early dawn, he stole out of the house and turned his steps toward the sea, if perchance its peaceful waters might soothe his unrest. He found the shore deserted, for even the fishermen had not yet returned from their toil of the night; and, with absorbed thought, he strolled on, heedless of his steps. Looking up suddenly, he saw just before him Jesus standing close upon the shore, looking out over the placid waters. The heart of Marcus gave a throb of joy as be beheld the man of whom his thoughts were full, but he stopped irresolute, shrinking from intruding upon his privacy. Jesus stood in silent meditation, looking with earnest and far-reaching gaze out over the placid waters of the sea, just blushing into roseate beauty beneath the first kisses of the morning sun.

The majesty of his mien, the beauty of his face and form, the divine light that to Marcus seemed to radiate from his entire being, spoke to him of the divine nature of the man before him, and he longed to throw himself at his feet and worship and adore. "I am always reminded when I look at him," so the thoughts of Marcus ran, "of the words of the prophet: 'Let thy garments be always white,' for his are spotless, at all times and in all places." Before he could withdraw silently, as he had contemplated doing, Jesus turned, and with an ineffable smile of welcome, held out his hand to him and drew the young man to his side.

"Thou, too, art seeking rest," he said gently; "surely it is in the scene before us," turning his face again toward the sea. A moment of silent thought, then Jesus said, "Shall we walk a little farther?"

"Gladly," Marcus answered. They walked along the shore, and the tiny waves sparkled and broke at their very feet. Then Jesus, turning, said:

"I am glad for this hour alone with thee, John Mark. There is much that I would say to thee, and the time for intercourse is short."

"Teacher, say on," said Marcus. "I am only too glad to hear aught from thy lips."

"There are three of my disciples I would have thee know well: Simon Peter and the brothers James and John, sons of Zebedee and Salome. They will be strength and comfort to thee in the days to come. Simon Peter, I am glad to see, thou dost already appreciate and love. He is cut from the rough granite, but is genuine. He is loyalty itself, but at times his impetuosity leads him to say or do that for which he is severely censured, and for which he repents in bitterness of spirit. And, Mark," said Jesus, looking into his eyes with beseeching tenderness, "if, in the near future, thou shalt hear of any such act upon his part in which I, too, am involved, because of thy love for me be gentle and uncensorious toward him. He will suffer enough from self-reproach; do not add to his heavy burden. He is a grand man, with sinews of oak and the heart of a dove.

"James is full of faith and zeal beyond any other one of my disciples, but he is modest and reticent until you know him well, when he becomes an anchor of strength in trouble. He shall taste the bitterness of the cup I drink, before any among you, but in so doing shall glorify my Father's name.

"What shall I say of John—so loyal, so pure, so gentle? He has all the grandeur of a man, with the simplicity and purity of a child. I never see him,"—and the eyes of Jesus grew inexpressibly tender—"but that I want to open my arms and fold him against my heart. Thou canst but love him, and he will comfort thee in thy need."

"I will remember all thou sayest," said Marcus, when Jesus finished speaking. "Why may I not accompany thee upon the journey of which thou didst speak, and so find opportunity for doing as thou hast said?"

"Nay," said Jesus, "thy present duty is to thy dear young wife and thine uncle Jairus. But in Jerusalem we shall meet again, and in the time to come thou shalt testify of me before the world." So saying, with a kindly smile he left him, and Marcus, turning, slowly retraced his steps.

All day long, while about his daily duties, the words of Jesus rang in the ears of Marcus and echoed in his heart. There was much he said that Marcus could not clearly understand. There was a hidden something underlying the spoken words that he fain would have made clear. What was the trouble to which he now so constantly alluded, as though to prepare them for some coming sorrow. He plainly spoke of his death being near. Did he really foretell it? Was there a foreshadowing of grand suffering in that death, from which the human part of his nature shrank? Could Peter explain these mysteries to him? Could John?

The evening of this same eventful day, as Marcus left the synagogue, he saw a man standing just outside the gates, as though awaiting the coming of someone, and a second look showed him that it was John, whom the Christ so loved. Approaching him eagerly with extended hand, Marcus said:

"I rejoice to meet thee thus; there is much that I would ask of thee. It draweth near the hour for the evening meal. I beg that thou wilt accompany me home and be my guest for the night."

"Most gladly," said John, showing evident pleasure at the request. "Our beloved teacher has so often spoken of thy worth, we long to know thee better, and I gladly embrace this opportunity for so doing."

As the two young men walked on together, in earnest, confidential conversation, their hearts were knit together as never before, and Marcus realized how Jesus could feel for John such tender and deep love. On reaching the palace, John was taken at once to a guest chamber, and every attention shown him that hospitality could demand. When, after the evening meal, as usual, they all ascended to the roof, the two young men drew apart from the others and conversed long and earnestly together. John told him much of Jesus' early history that was heretofore unknown to Marcus, and dwelt upon his wonderful power and his great sympathy and love for all mankind, that marked him as divine. Marcus told him of his anxiety lest evil was meditated against Jesus by the Council at Jerusalem, and John confirmed his worst fears and told him Jesus not only knew of their evil designs, but seemed almost to know that they would succeed, and finally compass his death; yet nothing could induce him to abandon his work, nor delay his journey to Jerusalem. Both men sat for some moments in sad reverie, when John said:

"It passes my comprehension how they can be so bigoted and so blind. The works that he has done so plainly show his divine power, that the man who denies it is either so hopelessly ignorant that he cannot see, or so willfully sinful that he will not." Then John narrated to Marcus many of the wonderful miracles that Jesus had wrought, and Marcus questioned and listened in wonder and awe.

"I think the healing of the maniac among the tombs the most wonderful of any I have witnessed," said John.

"More wonderful than the raising of the son of the widow of Nain, or—of my young wife?" asked Marcus, with a tender light in his eyes, as he looked over to the group where his wife was sitting in earnest conversation with her father and mother, a little removed from Marcus and John.

"Yes," said John, "for in each of these cases he but recalled the spirit to the tenement of clay that it had left; truly a miraculous act, but nothing to the first casting out of a legion of evil spirits to make room for the spirit of one worse than dead."

"How was it?" asked Marcus. "I think this is one of his miracles of which I have not heard. Tell me about it."

"It happened when we had gone with him to the country of the Gergesenes, just before the raising of your wife to life," said John. "Soon after we had landed upon the shore a man came rushing upon us from among the tombs, who was afflicted with the worst form of insanity ever known. For many years he had been beyond all human control, snapping asunder the chains with which they bound him as though they were silken threads, and often grievously wounding, if not actually killing, those who strove to control him. He tore all clothing from his body, gnashed with his teeth, and cut himself with the sharp stones of the crags over which he used to climb. His hair was long and matted like a lion's mane, and his nails upon both feet and hands had grown into claws, like an eagle's. His eyes were fierce and treacherous looking, and his white face and naked body were objects of terror to the entire country around. He came shrieking and leaping toward us, and at his demoniac yells, the affrighted people whom he met fled in every direction. He made direct for Jesus, who stood immovable, with his eyes fastened upon the frantic man. To our great surprise, even before Jesus spoke to him. he cried aloud,

'What have I to do with thee, thou Son of the most high God?' then threw himself at the feet of Jesus to worship him. Jesus said, as though addressing someone within him, 'I command thee to come out of him, thou unclean spirit.' Then the demoniac cried out beseechingly, 'I implore thee, torment us not before our time.' Jesus said to him, 'What is thy name?' And the man said, more calmly now, 'My name is Legion, for we are many; and we implore thee, if we must depart, that thou send us not entirely away, but let us go and abide in that herd of swine,' pointing to an immense herd feeding upon the hillside. Then occurred a strange thing. Jesus said, 'I command you to come out of the man at once, and never return to him; and you may go to the swine if you will, for you are all alike unclean.' Then the man fell upon the ground in violent convulsions, foaming at the mouth and tearing his long, unkempt hair from his head; and almost immediately afterward a violent commotion was seen in the herd of swine, that rushed madly hither and thither, and finally plunged headlong over a steep precipice into the sea, and were drowned. While this excitement was going on, Jesus whispered to us to take the man away and bathe and clothe him. And we led him away, and taking him to a secluded spot on the shore near by, gave him a cleansing bath, cutting away his matted locks and clawlike nails. And behold! on again reaching the shore a strange man handed us a bundle of clothing, including everything needful, even to the sandals for his feet. Whence the clothing came, we know not, for the man who brought them to us disappeared into the crowd with never a spoken word. The restored man, in answer to our inquiries, told us his name was Amos, that he had been a herder of cattle, and that his home was a short distance only from one of the cities of the Decapolis. When the multitude came, they found Jesus talking to Amos, who had at once gone to him and sat at his feet, and listened intently to every word he uttered. The appearance of this demoniac, 'clothed and in his right mind.' sitting at the feet of Jesus, claimed more of the attention of the crowd, I fear, than even the words of Jesus himself. Indeed, so frightened had they become at the wonderful things they had witnessed, that they besought Jesus to depart from their coasts, and at the conclusion of his discourse, he reentered the ship and bade adieu to their inhospitable shores. Someday, perhaps, they will understand how great the blessing they refused to receive. Amos begged to be allowed to accompany us on our return and follow Jesus wheresoever he went. But the Master said to him kindly, 'Not so, Amos, my friend; thy work is not with me. Go and tell thy friends what great things God hath done for thee, and publish everywhere the gospel of the Son of God.' I saw the keen disappointment Amos felt that he might not accompany Jesus, and my heart went out to him in great sympathy; so, on the impulse of the moment, I said, 'Teacher, if it seemeth good to thee, I would gladly do with Amos for a brief while, and with him bear the glad tidings of the gospel of peace.' Jesus turned upon me a look full of loving appreciation, as he said, 'Go with him, beloved; and the God of peace go with you both. I will await thee in Capernaum.' Then, turning to Amos, he laid a hand lightly upon each shoulder, as he said, 'It is not always those, my son, who are near me personally that do the most for me, but those who do my will and the will of the Father, who sent me. God hath done a great thing for thee, and thou, by showing it forth, canst do more for me among those who knew thee in thy former condition and who see thee now', than thou couldest ever do working with the many about me. It is a wonderful step from the darkness of demoniacism into the broad light of the gospel of peace: I send thee forth as the first messenger to tell of this truth to thy benighted brethren; and my spirit will go with thee to counsel and sustain thee withersoever thou goest. Thou art my servant, trusted and beloved from this time forth.' Then he laid his hands in blessing upon the bowed head of the man before him, whose face shone with the light of a great trust, even as Jesus talked. We went away together, Amos and I, and as we walked, he told me much of his early life. A great and holy joy seemed to possess him, and he was eager to begin his ministry for the God who had uplifted him. In answer to my inquiry as to when this great evil of his life befell him, he said with much feeling:

"'I was always a passionate, headstrong boy even in childhood, and was never willing to be guided by those older and wiser than I. I could not bear to be thwarted in my desires, and when my parents or teachers opposed my will, I would fly into violent outbursts of passion that amounted almost to frenzy. As I grew older, and my will grew stronger, these fits of frenzy became more frequent and continued longer, until in one of them I wandered away, and meeting with others of like condition, took up my abode in the tombs and lost all memory of time and place. I dimly recall, when pressed by hunger, now and then wandering back to my father's house; but their efforts to detain me always threw me into such paroxysms of rage that they finally came to barring all the doors and windows at my approach and hiding themselves from me, often managing to slip a basket of provisions to me through some door or window when I was not near. Once they drugged some wine placed in the basket, and while I lay in a stupor, dressed me and bound me with chains, hoping to recall me once more to myself. I remember this incident distinctly, because my mother was sitting beside me when I recovered consciousness from the wine. I loved my mother, and she could sometimes calm me, and my first feeling was one of pleasure when I saw her. But when I found that I was not only dressed but bound with chains, I tried to strike her, and the look of horror that crossed her face, stamped the incident indelibly upon my memory. I wrenched the chains asunder as though they had been threads, tore my clothing from my person in shreds, and tried my best to kill someone before I left the house; indeed, I believe I did kill one of the servants, but this may be one of my hallucinations.'"—Then, answering the desire of Marcus, John continued:

"I told him much of Jesus and his wonderful life, and before many hours we found ourselves approaching the city of Gadara. While it was still an hour's walk distant, Amos turned aside into an inclosure.[1] As we approached a humble but comfortable-appearing house, we saw, through the open door, the family gathered for the evening meal. They saw our approach, and the aged father rose to greet us, and bade us kindly welcome to the simple evening repast. They looked upon us both as strangers. The mother, too, arose and beckoned us to convenient seats. She looked into the face of her son with no sign of recognition. I saw that the heart of Amos was swelling with suppressed emotion, and as his mother stood for a moment near him, intent on hospitable duties, he bent over and whispered to her, 'My mother!' A startled look swept over her face, as, glancing quickly upward, her mother-eye penetrated the disguise, and with a sobbing cry, 'Amos, my son! my son!' she fell into his outstretched arms.

"Then ensued a scene such as I am wholly inadequate to describe. The family gathered about him in awe and wonder, and the old father, laying his trembling hand upon the arm of his son, peered with his failing eyes into his face, and falteringly said, 'Amos! Amos! Is it truly thou, my son?' And Amos, bending over, kissed his father on either cheek and said, with returning courage:

"'Aye, father, it is thy truant son returned this time, I trust to comfort and bless thy declining years.'

"'But, Amos,' said the still bewildered father, 'how comes all this? What has wrought this wonderful change? Who has given back to us the son that we believed was lost to us forever?' And the old man clung fondly to the arm of his son that still supported his weeping mother.

---

[1] Similar to a small farm in our country.

"'God, through his promised Messiah, hath wrought in me this marvelous thing. He it is who banished the demons from me, who gave me back my right mind, and best of all, my father, who hath shown to me the great light of the gospel of peace and truth.'

"The servants, who had been waiting upon their master at the evening meal, and had listened with wonder to these strange things, now hastened to all the neighboring houses, and one even ran as far as the city and spread the strange tidings—how Amos, the demoniac, had returned home, clothed and in his right mind; and the neighbors came hastening from far and near to see and hear the truth of these strange tidings. Soon the house was filled, and excited faces looked in at the doorways and through the windows. The face of Amos grew bright with joy, that so soon the way had opened for his ministry; and, turning toward them, he began:

"'Friends and neighbors, ye who knew me of old, when evil spirits had dominion over me, and behold me now as I stand before you here today, a strange thing I declare unto you, and one who stands beside me here will tell you still more marvelous things of which I have yet no knowledge, about Jesus of Nazareth, whom we believe to be the Messiah promised by the prophets of old.' Then he went on and told of his wretched life in the tombs, of his bondage to the evil spirits to whom he was in subjection, of his seeing Jesus afar off that day, and the spirits within him crying out that he was the Son of God! Of his marvelous deliverance, and his being sent home by Jesus to tell to them the truths of his great gospel.

"'I may well have told him,' he said to them, 'that my name was Legion, for a horde of evil spirits were my constant guests. The demon of anger, the demon of hatred, the demon of selfishness, the demon of malice, the demon of self-love, the demon of self-will, the demon of deceit, the demon of untruth, the demon of destruction, and a host of others of like nature, were always with me. An uncontrolled temper, an ungoverned will, will make a demoniac of any living creature. I say to you, my friends, that there are others besides Amos in the city of Gadara who are possessed of evil spirits! Who was it that raised his hand to slay his friend, because they differed on some trivial matter? Was it Nathan? Nay, it was the demon of anger that had found entrance to his heart. Who was it that robbed his brother of his inheritance, through some technicality of the law that enabled him to do so? Was it Timeus? Nay, but the evil spirits of avarice and selfishness that he harbored in his breast. Who fled from the home where she was encircled by purity and truth, and went with evil company and walked in strange ways? Was it Sara? or Judith? or Leah? Nay, but the demons of self-love, self-will and self-destruction that enticed them, and they yielded to the siren voices. I know all this, alas! too well, and I say unto you, beloved friends, there is only One upon earth whom these evil spirits fear, and that is Jesus of Nazareth. There is only one voice that they will obey: it is the voice of Jesus, who is the Christ, the Messiah, whom the prophets of old foretold. Before him "even devils fear and tremble," and all that is evil flees in affright. Call upon him to help you, and he will exorcise all of them from your hearts, and send, to fill their places, joy and peace and rest, such as my tongue can never make you understand. It was he who tore the black cloud from my life and permits me to look upon him in his beauty. It is he who sends me back, purified—vile creature that I was—to the beloved inmates of my long deserted home, and gives to my parents' arms the son they mourned as dead. Will you not also believe in him?'

"He spoke like one inspired, and the people hung upon his words, and many wept aloud and fell upon their faces and cried to God to send Jesus of Nazareth to deliver them from the bondage of the Evil One, that now they felt, for the first time, enslaved them.

"Then Amos turned to me and asked me to tell them the things I knew of Jesus. I spoke to them for more than an hour, and answered many questions asked; and many, that first night, believed that he was the Messiah. The father and mother of Amos—nay, more, all of his household—believed and rejoiced, and the evening meal was forgotten and the evening tasks were left undone, and much of the night was spent in thanksgiving and praise. And so began the work in the benighted country of the Gadarenes. I remained with him several days, laboring with him in all the Decapolis and the region round about, and then returned hither to the disciples."[2]

"Was it not upon this voyage," questioned Marcus, "that Jesus stilled the tempest? Were you in the boat at the time?"

"Yes," said John, "it was while we were crossing the lake on the way to Gadara that the scene occurred, and I, with the other disciples,

---

[2] Upon Jesus' return to this region, after visiting Tyre and Sidon, "There came unto him great multitudes, having with them the lame, blind, dumb, maimed and many others; and he healed them." Compare Matt. 15: 28-31 with Mark 7: 30-37. This was very probably due to the message of the healed demoniac.— [R. W. S.

was with him in the boat. It was a wonderful scene—one never to be forgotten. Jesus was very weary. The constant pressure of the multitude about him both day and night, and the continuous teaching, had exhausted him, and after entering the boat, he lay down upon a cushion in the stern and was soon asleep. When we were about half way across the lake, a sudden squall struck the boat, and in an instant all was confusion. The waves tossed it about like a dry leaf in the wind, and we all, greatly affrighted, clung to the mast or the gunwales for safety. But Jesus slept on as though in bed in his own house. We hesitated to disturb his peaceful sleep, but suddenly a wave, that seemed to us like a mountain, bore down upon us, flooding the front of the boat with water and sweeping overboard loose articles. Greatly affrighted, we cried out, 'Lord, save us! We perish!' And Simon Peter, I think it was, rushed at the peril of his life to where the Teacher still slept, and rousing him, cried: 'Carest thou not that we all perish?' Then Jesus, his eyes still heavy with sleep, sat up, and looking out over the foaming billows, seemed for the first time aware of the storm; and, turning his eyes calmly upon us, said sadly, 'Where is your faith?' Then he arose, and standing without support in the stern, looked upon the tempest that tossed his bright hair about his face and seemed trying to tear his white robe from his person. One moment he stood thus, in his majesty, then slowly raising his hand with a gesture of command, he said, in a tone of authority, 'Peace! Be still!' And the mad waves receded one upon the other, until the sea about us was as tranquil as you see it tonight," pointing as he spoke to the almost motionless waters of the moonlit sea before them. "We could see in the distance the water still foaming and dashing angrily about, but even that grew calm as he stood watching it; and soon a great calm lay upon the entire bosom of the sea. Turning to us then, Jesus said gently, 'Had your faith in the Father's power been strong enough, ye would only have had to ask him, in my name, to still the tempest, and it would have fled before you. Oh, ye of little faith!'[3] Then he again lay down upon his hard bed and slept peacefully. The men gathered in knots, and in low tones discussed the strange event and whispered among themselves, while stealing furtive glances at Jesus, and asked in awe, 'What manner of man is this, that even the winds and the sea obey him?' I stole over and sat down close beside Jesus, and yielding to an irresistible impulse, bent down and pressed my lips on his unsandaled feet. The action roused him, and looking at

---

[3] Compare John 14: 16.

me tenderly, he whispered, 'Beloved,' and lapsed into sleep again, with a divine smile playing about his lips.

"We had been so thrown from our course by the storm, and were all so weary and exhausted that we, too, slept, letting the boat drift, so that it was dawn before we reached our destination."

Long into the night talked these two devoted men, and their souls, like those of Jonathan and David, were closely knit together. The household had long retired before they parted, and beneath the stars they pledged fidelity to each other and loyalty to Him whom it was their privilege to honor and to serve. Two mornings thereafter, Jesus, with his disciples, started upon their missionary journey that was to end at Jerusalem in time for the Feast of the Passover, still some six months distant.

15

To live in hearts we leave behind
Is not to die.

~ Thomas Campbell.

There is no death! What seems so is transition:
This life of mortal breath
Is but a suburb of the life elysian,
Whose portal we call death.

~ Longfellow.

After Jesus and Marcus parted upon the seashore, in the early dawn, Jesus continued his way along the beach until he reached the outskirts of Magdala, when he left the lake; and, passing up the picturesque valley and through the gorge to the southwest, struck across the rolling hills in the direction of Nazareth.

He had no desire to publicly visit the place, since he had been openly rejected there, but he felt that he could not start upon his projected journey, which he well knew would end so tragically for him, without first seeing his mother and leaving with her thoughts that would afterward bring comfort to her heart.

When Jesus left Nazareth in the beginning of his ministry and made his home in Capernaum, his mother and brethren followed him thither; but Mary could not give up wholly the house at Nazareth, with its hallowed associations, so that part of her time was spent there in retirement; and there Jesus sought her as often as his duties would permit him to do so. At this time he avoided the highways, keeping to the fields for the most part, and reading in everything beautiful in nature the marks of his Father's love for his earthly children. The birds sang anthems of praise, and Jesus sang with them; the little mountain streams sparkled and danced and murmured joyously, and Jesus slaked his thirst in their sweet waters and let them ripple over his tired feet until he felt refreshed. The flowers bloomed everywhere, especially the lilies; and Jesus stooped and gathered them as he walked along, inhaling their fragrance and often pressing them to his face. By the time he had reached the outskirts of Nazareth and turned aside to his mother's modest home, he held a large cluster of flowers in his hand; and now, when almost at the threshold, he paused to examine anew an unusually large and perfect lily—the latest he had plucked. His mother, hearing and recognizing his step, came eagerly to the door to welcome him, and Jesus, looking up with a smile—holding the flowers toward her—said, as on another occasion, "Behold the lilies, how they grow! They toil not, they spin not; yet Solomon in all his glory was not arrayed like one of these!" He placed the flowers in her hand, and bending over, pressed his lips to her forehead, and then, with his arm caressingly around her, they entered the house together.

"It is long since I have seen thy face, my son," said Mary, looking up wistfully into the kind eyes above her.

"Yes, my mother, it is long. But thou knowest how urgent the business I have to do, and how I must work while the daylight lasts. No man knoweth when the night may come, and I would not have it find me with my work incomplete."[4]

They had seated themselves side by side, and Jesus still kept his arm protectingly around her, as she rested her head upon his shoulder. How in his tender heart he yearned to shield her from the deep sorrow that lay before her! If only she could be spared, and he could bear the anguish alone! But this he knew could not be, for the heart of the mother must suffer at the human agony of the son she so loved. They talked a little of many things of interest to them both, then Mary hastened to prepare the simple noontide repast, and Jesus went to the room for so many years exclusively his own, and after

---

[4] Compare John 9:4.

a refreshing bath, lay down upon his couch for a brief rest after his long, dusty journey. How strange it seemed to him that this was no longer his home! He loved the room: it was full of sweet memories for him. Opposite his couch, upon the wall, hung his first piece of workmanship, done under the direction and guidance of his foster-father, a set of shelves for his early books; and on them still stood several childish toys that he had fashioned in his boyhood for his younger brothers, now gone forth as men into the outer world. His mother treasured them because they were his workmanship. A case of drawers and a small table, also of his handiwork, stood on different sides of the room, and about each clustered happy memories.

As he lay thinking thus, a white dove settled upon the ledge of his open window with a soft cooing sound. Jesus looked tenderly upon it, and his thoughts ran back to the wonderful day when, upon the banks of the Jordan, the dove from the open heavens hovered above his head as he came up out of the water from his baptism. He went quietly to the open window, and the pretty bird did not shrink from the caressing touch of his hand. He raised it to his face, pressed his lips upon its snowy neck, and then held it without the casement that it might fly to its nest. But it only flew to the branches of the pomegranate tree overhanging the window, and still cooed its soft notes of love to the weary man within. Jesus turned from the window and stood a moment in silent contemplation, while a spasm of deep pain from some hidden thought contracted his face, colorless even to pallor; then, throwing himself upon his knees beside the couch, he lay across it with outstretched arms in an attitude of utter physical and mental exhaustion. Soon his lips began to move in prayer, and gradually the deathly pallor left his face, and he arose to a kneeling posture, and with uplifted face poured forth an agonized prayer for power to endure, for strength to suffer, for divine authority over all evil, for complete harmony with the divine will. As he prayed a great peace filled his heart, shone through his eyes and illumined his face, so that when he again went forth to his mother, she was filled with awe at the beauty of his countenance.

Together they sat at the simple repast, and the flowers he had gathered for her graced the board and filled the room with fragrance. Mary could not eat for looking at her son, and he, being filled with strength from a higher source, was not conscious of the need of food to sustain his body. Returning to the outer room, they sat together and conversed of many things in their past lives, and Jesus, again drawing his mother to his side, spoke of the pleasant memories his room awakened, especially the articles he had fashioned under Joseph's guidance. He told her of the gentleness of the dove that had alighted on the window ledge, but said no word of the memories it had awakened, nor of the awful struggle through which he had passed before he regained the peace for which he wrestled.

His mother asked him many questions concerning himself, then hesitatingly she said:

"My son, beloved and best of all my children, I have had many anxious hours concerning thee."

"Yes, my mother," said Jesus, gently drawing his arm more closely about her; "speak freely to me; I would know all."

"We hear so many alarming rumors of how evil men at Jerusalem seek thy life. The day thy brothers and I sought to approach thee when thou wast speaking, but could not get near because of the pressure of the multitude, we ourselves saw Aurelius of the household of Caiaphas accompanied by one of evil face, standing in the midst of the crowd not far from thee, eagerly watching thy every movement and listening to thy every word. Someone near whispered to us that they were waiting there for the purpose of killing thee when the crowd dispersed, and we tried to send a word of warning to thee. It was not our wish to disturb, but to save thee. Thy brothers, especially James and Jude, who are with thee the most, urge me constantly to entreat thee to withdraw, for a time at least, from thy present work, that this violent opposition may cease."

"Dost thou think this possible, my mother?—thou who knowest so well for what purpose I came into the world," asked Jesus, gently.

Mary's pale face flushed, and she hesitated a moment before she answered:

"But if they take thy life, my son, no one else can accomplish thy work."

"Most true; but they cannot take my life, sweet mother, till the work is finished for which I came. Even then, all they can do is to destroy this body; my life belongs to God— that they cannot touch."

They sat a brief while in silence, Jesus resting his cheek against his mother's forehead. Presently he said, as though dismissing these sad thoughts from their minds:

"I see thou hast still the little Egyptian lamp I so admired when a child. Has it ever ceased to burn?"

"Yes, I have it still, and the little flame has burned ceaselessly, just as I promised the princess who gave it to me, it should. It has, you know, two burners, and while one is being trimmed the other burns with

Marcus and Miriam

steady light." Jesus arose, and approaching the shelf upon which the lamp stood, examined it closely.

"It is of exquisite workmanship," he said.

"This outer case is very fragile and beautiful, made of this fine stained glass of many colors. And the tiny bronze lamp that holds the perfumed oil is wonderful in its beauty."

"Yes, and indestructible," said Mary, who was always proud of the dainty lamp that was given to her by an Egyptian princess many years before.

Jesus lifted the little bronze lamp out of its frail case and looked at it curiously. "What a steady, beautiful light it gives for so small a flame!" he said. "But behold the case! Where is its wonderful beauty now? It is only a very unsightly vase, possessed of no beauty whatever, no color but a dead leaden blue."

"That is because there is no light within," said his mother. "Restore the light, and it will be beautiful as before."

"I see," said Jesus, "it is the inner light that makes it beautiful."

"Yes," answered Mary. "The case is of little value without the light. That is why the light is never permitted to go out."

Jesus looked at her a moment wistfully before he said gently:

"Can you not see the similitude, my mother? This lamp is like the divine spark within us that we call life. When it is withdrawn, the body, which is like this case, has lost all of its beauty, and is cast aside as valueless. This, we say, is death. When you look into my eyes, that which looks out at you and responds to every word and thought is not the human eye itself, for, after death, the eye is still there in perfect organization, but it does not respond to you, it lies leaden and sunken, because the 'inner light'—the lamp—has been withdrawn for some wise purpose of the rather. That strange something that looks out at you through my eyes, like a prisoner through the bars of his cell, is my real self; and that no one can injure, for it is in the Father's care, and evil cannot reach it. Will you remember this, my mother, should evil counsels prevail and my body be given over unto death?"

"I will remember it, my son," said Mary, with deep emotion.

Then they again sat down together, and Jesus, reaching up to a shelf whereon the different books of the prophets always lay, took down the Psalms of David, and opening the book to the Ninety-first Psalm, with deep solemnity, read:

"He that dwelleth in the secret place of the Most High, shall abide under the shadow of the Almighty.

"I will say of the Lord, He is my refuge and my fortress: my God: in him will I trust.

"Surely, he shall deliver thee from the snare of the fowler, and from the noisome pestilence.

"He shall cover thee with his feathers, and under his wings shalt thou trust: his truth shall be thy shield and buckler.

"Thou shalt not be afraid for the terror by night; nor for the arrow that flieth by day; "Nor for the pestilence that walketh in darkness; nor for the destruction that wasteth at noonday.

"A thousand shall fall at thy side, and ten thousand at thy' right hand; but it shall not come nigh thee.

"Only with thine eyes shalt thou behold and see the reward of the wicked.

"Because thou hast made the Lord, which is my refuge, even the Most High, thy habitation; "There shall no evil befall thee, neither shall any plague come nigh thy dwelling.

"For he shall give his angels charge over thee, to keep thee in all thy ways.

"They shall bear thee up in their hands, lest thou dash thy foot against a stone.

"Thou shalt tread upon the lion and adder: the young lion and the dragon shalt thou trample under feet.

"Because he hath set his love upon me, therefore will I deliver him: I will set him on high, because he hath known my name.

"He shall call upon me, and I will answer him: I will be with him in trouble; I will deliver him, and honor him.

"With long life will I satisfy him, and shew him my salvation."

As he read, his mother sat with folded hands and downcast eyes, and as she listened, a sweet peace stole into her heart and overspread her face. He closed the book, replaced it on the shelf, and together they knelt in prayer. Jesus offered up a short, earnest petition to God that he would lead them in all their ways, that he would comfort and bless them and all dear to them, even as he would comfort and bless his children everywhere; that he would give them courage and strength for any trial that might lie before them, and make them show forth his glory at all times and in all places, so that men beholding his glory shining through their lives might be drawn to him, the living Father of all.

When he arose he placed his arm once more about his mother, as he said, "Thinkest thou not, my mother, it would be well if thou wouldest refrain from going up to Jerusalem to the Feast of the Passover this year?"

But Mary, looking into his eyes with a brave though sad smile, answered:

"Whatever of suffering lies before my son, he shall always have the comfort of knowing his mother is beside him."

Jesus stooped suddenly and pressed an earnest, tender kiss of parting upon her lips, and turning, passed from the house forever.

After walking rapidly a little distance, he paused as though to take a farewell of the beautiful spot for so many years his home. There lay the lovely valley beneath him, with its flowery hedges and its verdant fields, and the narrow pathway, flower-bedecked, that led from the valley to the village nestling against the stony hillside. He had ascended a little way, so that the village lay in a hollow at his feet. He saw the synagogue wherein, as a boy, he had received instruction, and where, in later years, when the Spirit of God was upon him, he stood up and read:

> "He hath anointed me to preach good tidings to the poor;
> He hath sent me to proclaim release to the captives;
> And recovering of sight to the blind;
> To set at liberty them that are bruised;
> To proclaim the acceptable year of the Lord."

He remembered how, offended by his plain teaching, they had risen against him, and would have cast him headlong down the hill upon which he stood, had not God protected him from their fury. He now saw the women drawing water from the well by the roadside, and the children playing about the fountain where he himself as a child had played. Then he turned for a last look at the home he was leaving forever. There it lay on the outskirts of the village, half hidden by flowering vines, and surrounded by the tall palms and the flowering orange and pomegranate. There he knew his mother sat in solitude— for her daughters had married and left her, her husband Joseph had long slept with his fathers, and her sons deserted Nazareth forever after its cruel rejection of Jesus. But there were too many hallowed associations connected with the place for Mary to desert it wholly. Jesus, as he looked, saw the seat beneath the trees where he so oft had sat to con [*sic*] his lessons; he saw the window of the room that the greater part of his earthly life he had called his own, and marked the scarlet blossoms of the pomegranate making festoons with the green leaves about the casement. In the background he saw the shop where he had worked with his foster-father Joseph, and he fancied he could almost see the kindly face of the man looking from the latticed window. Full of tender memories, he turned away and hastened toward Capernaum, for the shadows were falling, the day was done, and there was nothing henceforth for him in Nazareth.

16

The name of Jesus is not only light, but also food: it is likewise oil, without which all of the food of the soul is dry; it is salt, unseasoned by which whatever is presented to us is insipid; it is honey in the mouth, melody in the ear, joy in the heart, medicine to the soul; and there are no charms in any discourse in which his name is not heard.

~ Bernard.

When Jesus and his disciples started upon that ever memorable tour that was to end only at Calvary, they first went to Tyre, then to Sidon, then visited all the cities of the Decapolis, where the many who had heard the testimony of the restored demoniac thronged to Jesus for healing and instruction. Then, passing hastily through Capernaum, they went to the neighborhood of Ceasarean Philippi. For some reason they seem not to have entered that town, but to have visited only the lesser neighboring cities and villages; then, turning southward, they pursued their journey toward Jerusalem. All along the way the people flocked about Jesus and regarded him with reverence and love. The little children clung to his hands and held to his robe, and not infrequently the tiniest among them was carried in his arms, his little cheek pressed lovingly against the Teacher. Many were the wonderful works performed by him upon this journey. The sick were healed, the lepers were cleansed, the lame were made to walk, the eyes of the blind were opened, the ears of the deaf were unsealed; and, best and most glorious of all, the poor had the gospel of the kingdom of heaven preached to them.

Once only did Jesus return to Capernaum, and then but for a few hours. It is not recorded for what purpose he went, but he entered not the synagogue, nor taught, nor did he at that time there do any wonderful work. Jairus and Marcus knew of his coming, and met him on the highway outside of the city, and took him to the palace, where he abode during his brief stay. Again they all sat together on the roof in the starlight, and again he spoke plainly to them of his approaching death, and showed to them comforting glimpses of the "many mansions" in his Father's house.

Marcus accompanied him on his return, and Miriam was later to go with her parents to Jerusalem, so as to be there a little in advance of Passover Week. She had more than one comforting talk with the Teacher she so loved, for Jesus, seeing the anguish of her heart at his approaching death, would not leave her comfortless. He bade her remember always that whatever she might see him suffer was necessary for the opening of the gate into his Father's kingdom, where she, too, would sometime come to share his glory. And she promised to be brave and strong, and remember all that he had said to her. Alas! how little she knew the agony of the way before him, or how great the strength that she herself would require to keep that promise.

Never, through all of his after life, did Marcus forget the days that he journeyed alone with Jesus, nor the blessed experiences of the way. The other disciples, who had accompanied Jesus to Capernaum, walked together a little in advance of Jesus and Marcus part of the time, as they resumed their journey, so that the two were practically alone, and conversed with great freedom together.

Through a country infested by robbers of the worst order, Marcus felt no fear by day, no dread by night. He seemed to live in a charmed circle that evil could not enter. Is it not ever thus with those who walk with Jesus, the Son of God?

In one of the villages through which they passed, lived a poor woman whose name was Leah, and because of her great infirmity she was widely known as "Crooked Leah." While still but a child her shoulders had been made to bear heavy and grievous burdens, so that, little by little, the tender spine had yielded to the unwonted pressure and become curved and bent, until, when full-grown, she seemed no larger than a child. But, though the poor, maimed and distorted body was a sight sad to look upon, the soul that it incased was pure and gentle and lovely as the morning. Debarred, by her infirmity, from the frivolities of life, her thoughts had turned to nobler, better things, and her face reflected the beauty of the soul within. Everyone felt kindly toward the poor woman who for eighteen long years had been bowed and broken with this dreadful infirmity. Leah had heard much of the wonderful prophet of Nazareth, and in her inmost heart accepted him as the promised Messiah; so, when she heard that he was to pass through the village in which all of her life she had lived, and that he would probably teach in their synagogue, she determined, if possible, to both see and hear him. It had never occurred to her to ask help from him for her own infirmity—that she had long ago learned to accept with patience—but she did want to hear him tell of the "house of many mansions" in his Father's kingdom. So one Sabbath morning, when she heard that he was approaching the village, she crept into the synagogue and stood near one of the great pillars, that she might be protected from the surging crowd that she knew would fill the place to see One whose fame was filling every mouth.

When Jesus entered the synagogue, the first form that he saw was that of the deformed woman, and the purity and sweetness of the patient face that looked so wistfully and eagerly toward him, appealed at once to his heart of tender compassion. The poor neck, he saw, was sadly and cruelly twisted, in order to get the eyes high enough to look into the face of the prophet she revered and loved. The love and adoration he saw in those eyes met with a quick response, for, crossing at once to where she stood, he laid his hand upon her and said gently:

"Daughter, be loosed from thine infirmity."

Instantly she stood tall and erect, a comely woman, who threw herself in adoration at his feet and praised him for his wondrous mercy.

The people crowded about him in awe and wonder, and many believed on [sic] Jesus for this act of mercy. The ruler of the synagogue—ah! the ruler, clothed in a little brief authority—both feared and hated Jesus because of his wonderful power over evil of every kind, and because of his great influence over the multitude wherever he went, so he seized this opportunity of persecuting him for healing this poor unfortunate.

"There are six days in which men ought to work," said he to the multitude; "come and be healed in these, and not on the Sabbath day."

Then Jesus, with indignation, said to him, "Hypocrite! Do you not loose your ox or your donkey from the stall, and lead him away to be watered upon the Sabbath? And shall not this poor woman, whom

Satan hath bound for, lo, these eighteen years, be loosed also upon the Sabbath?"

And the ruler was shamed into silence, and all the people rejoiced that Jesus had triumphed. Then Leah, who had listened in amazement to the rebuke of the ruler to this great prophet, again approached him, and with tearful, uplifted eyes, said tremblingly:

"Teacher, take back thy wonderful gift of mercy to thy servant. Rather than harm should come to thee, I would bear the pain and humiliation forever. The remembrance of thy love to me would make the burden light."

Jesus, looking upon her tear-stained, earnest face, saw nothing of the coarse servant's garb she wore, nor cared for the rude sneering of the ruler and his followers. He laid his hand tenderly upon her head as he said, "In my Father's house are many mansions. Thou, my daughter, hast won thy place therein. Fear nothing, but go in peace." And she departed with a heart filled with rejoicing. Jesus, turning to John, his beloved disciple, who stood near him, said:

"Scarce three days ago, ten lepers were cleansed of their loathsome and fatal disease and restored to the rights of home and citizenship, from which, by that dread disease, they were debarred. Thou knowest that one alone of the ten returned to thank me for God's mercy to them. One alone was grateful enough to promise to live henceforth a better life; yet this poor woman, whose soul was white within the distorted body, even in the first glad moments of her freedom, comes and begs me to recall the mercy shown, lest evil may come to me for the act. This, John beloved, is gratitude such as is seldom found, and of such white souls is the kingdom of my Father composed."

Thus from day to day and from hour to hour, was the journey pursued, which, though long and circuitous, was bringing Jesus nearer to the cross on which he was to suffer. He knew that it was there, he knew that it would rear its ghastly head on Calvary at the appointed time, yet steadfastly he went forward, step by step, blessing and helping all with whom he came in contact, never forgetting, yet never shrinking from the dread fate that lay before him.

On the eastern slope of the Mount of Olives, about two miles east of Jerusalem, lay the beautiful village of Bethany, surrounded by its groves of dates and olives. It was there that the two sisters, Mary and Martha, with their brother Lazarus, lived; and in their lovely home Jesus often stopped when visiting Jerusalem, for he had no friends whom he loved more tenderly than these three. It was this Mary, who, after

Lazarus' resurrection, anointed Jesus' head and feet with the costly spikenard ointment, and wiped his feet with the long silken tresses of her hair, and of whom, when some would have found fault with her for so doing, Jesus said tenderly, "Let her alone; she is but anointing me in preparation for my burial."

Lazarus and Martha and Mary loved Jesus for the wonderful depth and sweetness of his divine nature, and for that indefinable something that drew all men unto him, save those who, in their evil hearts, sought to destroy him. Lazarus became one of his most devoted followers and friends, and next to John, he was beloved of Jesus. In his frequent visits to their home in Bethany, if Mary could but sit at his feet and listen to his converse with her brother, she was supremely happy and content. He had become the center of her world, and there was no happiness for her apart from him.

Martha also loved Jesus, but her ambition was to surround him with creature-comforts during his stay with them, to prepare dainty food to set before him, and to adorn the room prepared for him with fragrant flowers and perfumed linen. She, too, loved to listen to his gracious and instructive conversation, but she felt that the duties of hospitality were paramount to her own pleasure, and in this way she lost much of the blessing her sister gained. This fact she finally realized. For, once, when doubly busy with household duties, as she passed through the room where Jesus and Lazarus sat conversing, and saw Mary, full of happy content, sitting listening at their feet, she paused and called aloud to Jesus, "Master, dost thou care that Mary leaveth me to perform all the household work alone? Wilt thou not bid her come and help me serve?" And Jesus looked up into the face before him, pleasant and loving in spite of her protest, and answered her in tender reproof: "Martha, Martha! Thou art anxious and troubled about many things, dear child. Why not choose, as Mary has done, the better part, and learn of the things that tell of the blessed life that no man can take from thee?"

Mary, who loved her sister dearly, sprang to her feet, and hastening to her. said: "Come, dearest Martha; come and hear of the wonderful life of which Jesus tells. Come, and afterward I will help thee with the work that seems so trivial to me when Jesus is here."

"Yes, Martha, come," said Jesus, reaching his hand invitingly to her. And Martha, very willing to be persuaded, came and sat down by Jesus. He talked to them of the wonderful river of life, that flowed from beneath his Father's throne, that washed away all sin and uncleanness and gave eternal life to all that would drink of its healing waters.

"But, teacher," said Martha, practical in all things, "with all of our desire to enter this perfect life, how are we to grow into it with our imperfect natures? With such as thou it is no mystery, for thou wert pure and good from the beginning, but we—alas! there is no good in us!"

"Thou hast said the word, my child; grow into it step by step. No grain or fruit is born perfect into the world. We place the seed of corn in the ground and cover it with the mold. The rain falls upon it, and the sun warms the earth above it, and after a time the clod of clay is broken, and the tiny blade appears. First the seed, then the blade, then the full ripe ear. I would plant the seed of God's dear love in your hearts; he waters and warms it with the rain of his mercy and the sun of his loving kindness, and in due time, the Holy Spirit pronounces it as ripe for the garner of the Lord. But only by patience and care can the harvest come."

In after days they dwelt in loving remembrance upon these words so full of encouragement and love.

17

"Behold how he loved him."

Jesus, with his disciples, and his devoted follower, Marcus, now made a missionary tour of Perea, the country lying east of the Jordan. The Jews had become so violent towards him that he went into this voluntary retirement across the Jordan in order to avoid being arrested by them before the time which he knew had been set apart by the Father for the closing scene in the drama of his mortal life. In the course of this journey, they came to Bethabara, only a little distance south of the Sea of Galilee, and he did there many wonderful things that proved to the people that he was truly the Messiah whom John the Baptist had in that very place first declared him to be. During one of the most memorable days of his ministry there, word was brought to him that his beloved friend, Lazarus, of Bethany, was very ill, and with the word, came an urgent plea from Mary and Martha, the sisters of Lazarus, that Jesus would hasten to them and save the brother they so loved. To the surprise of all, especially of his disciples, who knew how well-beloved of Jesus both Lazarus and his two sisters were, he delayed his departure for two days after the message came, sending word to Mary and Martha that this sickness of their brother was "not unto death, but for the glory of God."

How strange this message must have seemed to them, coming as it did from one whom they trusted and loved as they did Jesus, for already, when it was received, Lazarus was not only dead, but buried.[5]

"Oh!" said Martha to her sister, as they wept beside the lifeless body of their brother, "Why does he seem to have forgotten us now in our hour of greatest need?"

And Mary whispered through her tears, "He has not forgotten us; something tells me that when he comes he will show us clearly that this trial, though so grievous to us now, will really in some way 'show forth the Father's glory,' as he has sent us word. If only he would come!" she moaned. "If only he would come!" Two days after the message was received by Jesus at Bethabara, he said to his disciples: "Come, let us now return again to Judea." But Peter—impetuous Peter—said: "Lord, why return into Judea when thou knowest those are there who constantly seek thy life?" Jesus answered, "Nothing can harm me without the Father's will. I have no fear, so long as I know I am in the line of my duty. Lazarus sleepeth and I go to awaken him."

"Then," said some of his disciples, "if he sleep, Lord, he doeth well; so why endanger thy life without cause?"

Then Jesus, seeing that they could not understand, said to them plainly, "Lazarus is dead, and I am glad for your sakes that I was not there, to the intent that ye may believe; nevertheless, let us go unto him."

Thomas, though one of the doubting, and at times, unbelieving disciples, was much devoted to the Master, and at once his tender heart rejected the thought of allowing this Master whom they all so loved to go into danger alone, so he burst forth, with almost Peter's impetuosity, saying, "If he will go, let us go also, that we may die with him."

Thus, accompanied by his disciples, Jesus started on his return to Bethany. He well knew the dangers that awaited him, he knew the Jews were lying in wait, not only to oppose him, but, if possible, to kill him; but he could not resist the cry of these dearly beloved friends, though, to all outward seeming, he had neglected them in the time of greatest need.

It was in the early morning that they approached Bethany in Judea. Even then, Jesus did not go to the house of Lazarus, that had so often been his home in his journeyings, but stopped outside the village, and said to John: "Go secretly to the home of Mary and Martha, and say that I am waiting for them at this place. They will understand and come to

---

[5] Obviously, if Jesus only delayed two days, yet found Lazarus dead four days, he could not have arrived in time to save his life if he had started at once. The delay, then, only accentuated the miracle of resurrection.—R. W. S.

me." John hastened to do his bidding, and as he approached the house, not far distant, he found Martha, who could not neglect even in the midst of her sorrow her household duties, engaged in preparing the morning meal, and he said to her quietly, that others might not hear, "The Master has come and would see both you and your sister."

"Oh," said Martha, dropping at once the work upon which she was engaged, "take me to him quickly!" And she hastened to throw herself at the feet of Jesus with the cry, "Oh, teacher, hadst thou been here my brother had not died! Why didst thou forget us in our sorrow? But I know that even now God will do for thee whatever thou wilt ask."

Jesus, with his heart full of pity, replied, "Thy brother shall rise again."

"Yes," answered Martha, "I know that he shall rise at the resurrection on the last day; but, oh, why were we to lose him now!"

Jesus said softly to her, "I am the resurrection and the life; he that believeth on me, though he die, yet shall he live. Believest thou this, Martha?"

"Yea, Lord, I do believe thou art the Christ, the Son of God."

Jesus answered her tenderly, "Waver not in thy faith, and all shall yet be well. Where is Mary that she came not also with thee?"

Then Martha, who felt a little conscience-stricken that in her haste she had left the house without even telling her sister, hastened back, and finding that many friends had come and were sitting in the room with Mary in order to comfort her in her sorrow, she went in quietly and whispered, "The teacher has come, and calleth for thee."

Then Mary, without a word to those about her, rose hastily, accompanied Martha from the room, and together they returned to where Jesus was awaiting them. Mary, when she saw Jesus, did even as Martha had done, falling down at his feet and crying unto him, "Lord, if thou hadst been here, my brother had not died."

Mary's friends, who had been watching with her in the house, were somewhat startled by her sudden departure, and they said to one another, "She has certainly gone to the grave of Lazarus, to weep there. Let us accompany her, that possibly we may comfort her in her sorrow'." But, when they followed closely after the two sisters, they found it was to Jesus they had gone, not to their brother's grave, and when they saw Mary at the great teacher's feet, weeping, they also wept and sorrowed with her. Then was Jesus deeply troubled; his heart ached for these women who had been for so many years his friends, and he said, with deep sympathy in every tone, "Where have ye laid him?"

Then the two sisters, one upon either side, drew him gently forward and whispered, "Come and see." As he walked with them, deep sobs came from each broken heart, and Jesus' own heart was torn with anguish that they should so suffer, and tears of sympathy chased each other down his cheeks.

The Jews who were with them whispered one to the other, "Behold how he loved him!" And some said, "Could not this man, who they say has so much power with God, have saved his friend, whom he seems to so love, from death?"

When they reached the tomb, they gathered about the entrance, even the sisters thinking that Jesus had come to do reverence to the memory of the dead. For a moment he stood silent and sad. Then lifting up his face he looked steadfastly for a moment into the heavens. Turning to the men who were standing near, he said, in a tone of command, "Take away the stone."

Mary was watching eagerly to see what he would do. But when Martha heard his command, her natural horror of the dead, even though dear to her in life, overcame her, so that she said, "Nay, nay, teacher; he hath already lain four days in the tomb; let them not disturb him now."

In reply, Jesus said softly unto her, "Said I not that, if thou believest, thou shouldest see the glory of God?" And his voice, so full of strange power, caused her to step back and hold her peace. Then once more Jesus said: "Take away the stone." And they took it away. Again Jesus, lifting his voice, said: "I thank thee, Father, that thou hast heard me, and that thou wilt for thine own glory show forth thy love and power." And Jesus, looking steadfastly into the darkness of the sepulcher, cried with a loud voice, "Lazarus, come forth!" And the young man, with his face bound with a napkin[6] and his winding sheet about him, stepped to the entrance of the tomb and stood looking out upon the multitude. But what strange sight is this? Although bound from head to foot in the clothes of the grave, his face is not that of a dead man, but the skin is as roseate as in health; and his eyes—that look with inquiry upon the great teacher—are bright and full of intelligence. Then Jesus said, "Loose him, and let him go."

Most of the multitude who had gathered about the tomb to see what Jesus would do, when they saw Lazarus come forth cried aloud, "It is a spirit!" and fled, affrighted, from the tomb. Martha, with dilated eyes and face pallid with terror, crouched upon the ground and gazed from

---

[6] Tied under the jaws, to keep the mouth closed, not over the eyes.

Jesus to her brother with an appalled look; but Mary, kneeling with clasped hands uplifted, whispered in an ecstasy of feeling, "He is the Christ! He is the promised Messiah! He is—he is the Christ!"

Jesus stepped forward and put his arms about the neck of the friend he so loved, and said, "For the Father's glory hath this been permitted." Then he unbound the napkin from about the face of Lazarus, that he might be wholly free, for those who had essayed to obey the command "Loose him, and let him go," in their great terror had left it still bound about him, and had slipped away with the others who had fled.

Lazarus, dropping upon his knees, kissed again and again the sandaled feet of Jesus, who, tenderly raising him, presented him alive and well to his astonished and bewildered sisters.

Together they returned to the village, and Jesus went with Mary and Lazarus and Martha to their pleasant home; for, even in the face of the great danger that threatened him, he could not forsake them in an hour like this.

And what a reunion that was between the four! One coming back to them from beyond the walls of the other life. Long they sat together, into the hours of the night, after the simple evening repast was over, for Jesus well knew, though they knew it not, that this would be his last quiet visit with them upon earth. When next he came, it would be at the approach of the Passover Week, and thenceforward to the journey to Calvary danger and death would constantly confront him and terrify and sadden the friends who loved him most. Peter and James and John, alone of the disciples, together with Marcus, were with him in the home of Lazarus, the others having retired to the little camping-ground outside the village. It was here that Jesus spoke to them more plainly of his approaching death, and turning, said to Lazarus:

"Thou mayest tell them whether or not the life beyond the grave is anything to dread."

Lazarus, with an ineffable look of peace upon his face, said:

"Oh, my friend, my Master, thou, too, knowest."

Jesus did not stay until the morning, lest the Jews should seek him even in that place of peace, for many who had witnessed the raising of Lazarus had been absolutely convinced by this miracle that Jesus was the Christ, and publicly proclaimed their faith, as they told the wonderful story. But some, alas! with hatred in their hearts, bore the story to the chief priests and Jews, as new evidence of his seeking to draw the people from the true faith to which they owed allegiance.

Marcus and Miriam

While the stars were yet shining, Jesus, together with his disciples, journeyed to Ephraim, where he remained quiet during the short time intervening before his final return to Jerusalem.

18

> The love I bear for thee is deep and true;
> Peril and toil, even death, I'll gladly meet
> If I may only worship at thy feet,
> Or lowliest tasks in thy blest service do.
>
> —R. R. S.

When on this last peaceful visit to Bethany, the hours so full of joy had slipped by almost unheeded, and as the evening repast was over, Jesus arose and signaled to Marcus to accompany him outside the cottage. The others, understanding well that Marcus was to remain no longer in the company who would go with Jesus to Ephraim, the little City of the Plain, and realizing how much a little privacy would mean to Marcus, if not to Jesus also, refrained from interrupting them, and they went forth together to a retired spot.

"John Mark," said Jesus, tenderly, "I shall miss thee at our nightly gatherings, but it is well that thou shouldest precede me to Jerusalem. There is much that must be done that only thou canst do for me."

"Teacher," replied the young man, with deep emotion, "thou knowest how gladly I lay my life, my all, for service at thy feet. Speak only, and say to me plainly, what thou wouldest have me do, and with my life I will perform it."

"Thy father, thou well knowest, has long been a dear and trusted friend to me. For his sake I would not let this be publicly proclaimed. It would only have caused for him the hatred of the Sanhedrin, and have done for me no good. Hence I have thought it wiser and better that our deep friendship for one another should be secret as well as fervent. Not even John and Peter, who know so well the most that I do, know anything whatever of this. I do not think they would recognize thy honored father should they meet him, much less do they dream that he and I have many plans in common, that he alone has carried forward for me. Say to him, when thou seest him, John Mark, that I have still one last favor to ask of him."

"Thou knowest, my teacher, how gladly all that thou desirest he will hasten to do; only speak the word, that I may bear it to him."

"Say to him, beloved son, that this last favor I would ask of him he himself long ago suggested to me, little dreaming in what manner it would be received. Once and again hath he said to me in the past: 'In the upper portion of my house there is a banqueting-room that I have long desired to fill with guests to honor thee.' But I have always bidden him wait, not desiring to call the attention of the Jews to his interest in me. Say to him that now he may prepare that upper chamber for my use, and in it I will eat with my disciples the Passover Supper. But with my disciples only, John Mark; I may not even bid thee come, nor thy beloved father. Hereafter, thou wilt know the reason for this, and thou wilt trust me without further explanation. This banquet must, for the present, be kept wholly secret; the Jews must not even know that I am to enter thy father's house. In one of his rooms he hath shown me an earthen pitcher, most artistically and beautifully decorated. Say to him to send a man servant with this pitcher to the fountain at the end of the street, at the hour preceding that fixed for the supper. I will direct John and Peter to go to the fountain, and when they see a man bearing such a pitcher as I shall describe, to follow him until he reaches his master's house. They will not know that it is to thy father's house that he is going. They shall ask for 'the goodman of the house,' and shall say to thy father, when they are brought into his presence, 'The teacher desireth to eat the Passover with his disciples in thy banqueting-room;' and let him lead them thither. Thou wilt remember all this faithfully in thy heart, John Mark, and as I said before, the time will come when thou wilt remember and understand all that I have said."

Marcus bent over and kissed the hand of Jesus, and his voice choked with emotion as he responded:

"I will remember; I will perform all that thou hast said, and when the time shall come, I will be there and see that all thy wishes and desires are carried out."

Then Jesus, laying his hands a moment in blessing upon the young man's head, bent over and pressed his lips upon his cheek. And so they parted, Jesus to go to the City of the Plain, and Marcus to Jerusalem.

After parting from Jesus, Marcus bent his steps toward Jerusalem, and upon entering the city, hastened at once to the house of his father. He found him at home, surrounded by guests—merchants who had come with a caravan to the city and had hastened to see their early friend, the "goodman of the house," with whom they were now concluding their evening repast. They all greeted Marcus with much pleasure, for he was ever a favorite with his father's friends. Marcus sat for a little while in their midst, listening to their conversation, which was full of life and hilarity, but which grated most discordantly upon his feelings, coming as he had from scenes of such a different nature than those now before him. After a short time, he excused himself to his father and his father's friends on the plea of weariness, and retired to the privacy of his own room. Here his father, after the guests had departed, sought him, and Marcus, with great earnestness, availed himself of the opportunity to tell him of the many wonderful scenes through which he of late had passed. He was glad of this private interview with his father, and closing the door of his room, so as to make their privacy more complete, he narrated his last conversation with Jesus, and delivered the messages that had been sent by Jesus to his friend, the father of Marcus.

The "goodman of the house" seemed greatly interested in all that his son now told him. In answer to an earnest inquiry from Marcus, he admitted that he had long been an intimate friend of Jesus, though privately.

"Where did you first meet him, and how?" inquired Marcus. "It never occurred to me that you could know him, until Jesus himself told me at the house of Jairus."

"Well," said his father, in a contemplative mood, "I have for some years been very much dissatisfied with the teachings of the Sanhedrin, and believed there was a better way, if we could only find it. One day, in coming from the hill country, I chanced upon a throng of people whom Jesus was addressing, and stopping on the outskirts of the crowd, I listened attentively to all that he might say. I was surprised and pleased at the purity and beauty of the doctrine he taught, and I said to myself, 'This surely is a true prophet, and he is teaching the truths for which I so long have sought.' Several times thereafter, at intervals, I heard him, and more than once tried to meet him personally. But, in some way, and as I now find, not accidentally, he managed to evade me, and it was not until some months after first hearing him that we met one night, as I was journeying to Capernaum. I saw him walking with some of his disciples, on the way there, and alighting from my chariot, which I ordered should return to Jerusalem, I drew near and attached myself to his party, with the usual traveler's salutation. His disciples, as I found was their usual custom, walked on a little in advance, when they saw that Jesus had turned to me, thus leaving us at liberty to converse in freedom. I told him how pleased I was to have this opportunity to meet him, how I had sought to know him, how I had listened to him more than once as he taught the people, that I believed the doctrine he taught was true, and that it was my desire to attach myself to him henceforth in all of his goings. At this he turned to me with a look of ineffable tenderness upon his face, and stretching forth his hand, he said, 'I have long known this, David, my friend, but I was not willing that thou shouldest sacrifice thy wellbeing and, perchance, thy life, for me.' I was more than astonished that he should call me thus familiarly by name, and I at once responded, 'I should not consider it a sacrifice to do anything that would advance thy cause.' We talked together earnestly for some time, and then he said to me, 'David, my friend, canst thou not see that there are many ways in which thou canst serve me, provided our friendship is not publicly known? But, by attaching thyself to me, thou wilt at once be identified with my cause, and any evil that may come to me would likewise come to thee. This I cannot permit. But, if thou wilt be my friend, there are ways in which thou canst help me, without the knowledge of others, until the time shall come when our friendship for one another can be known.' He talked so earnestly that I could but see the wisdom with which he spoke, and promised I would abide by anything he should desire. And so it came to pass that, as we neared Capernaum, I entered by the western gate and left Jesus and his disciples to proceed along the shore. Since then, in many ways, he has called upon me for favors, that I could do only by having it unknown that we were personal friends. He has always promised that when the time came, he would call upon me for one favor, beyond which I could ask no greater, and now I see his meaning: he would eat the Passover Supper with his disciples in my banqueting chamber. It shall all be as he desires."

"Yes," answered Marcus, "it shall all be as he desires."

A few days after Marcus' arrival in Jerusalem, Miriam and her parents joined him, desiring to spend some little time in the city before the Feast of the Passover.

One evening, as they were walking down one of the narrow streets, they stopped to examine some strange curios in a little shop; and, while they were intently observing them, a group of noisy men, headed by Aurelius, of the household of Caiaphas, entered the shop. Aurelius at once perceived that Marcus and Miriam were there, but made no sign, proceeding boisterously with the conversation upon which he and his companions were engaged when entering the shop.

" What wilt thou then do?" asked one of his companions.

"Do?" said Aurelius, with a brutal laugh. "We will make this wonderful Nazarene prophet show the divinity of his power. I tell you it will be a more wonderful sight than even the gladiatorial races. Thou must not fail to see it, Perseus."

Marcus hurriedly drew Miriam from the shop, and as they passed out, Aurelius said sneeringly, in a tone loud enough for them to hear: "There go two of the most devoted followers of this Nazarene."

"Is not that the daughter of Jairus, whom Jesus raised from the dead?" questioned one of his companions.

"The dead!" said Aurelius, with a sneer. "She was only feigning death, and anyone could have awakened her. Jesus himself said, 'She is not dead, but sleepeth,' and it is only such fanatics as these you see before you who insist that he performed a miracle."

At this, there was a brutal laugh all around, and Marcus, with a flushed face, drew Miriam into a side-street and out of the way quickly as possible. There could be no quarrel in the presence of his wife; besides, alas! what would it avail. Jesus himself had declared that the hour for his death had come, and any interference on their part might only make it more terrible for him.

Miriam, white and very quiet, walked by her husband's side, until they reached the doorway of his father's house, when, looking up with a pitiful glance into the face of her husband, she cried:

"Oh, Marcus! What will they do with him?" He drew her gently within the entrance of the house, then said earnestly to her:

"We must remember all that he taught us in those two wonderful nights that we spent together upon the roof of the palace."

"Yes," said Miriam, the light springing into her eyes, "we must remember."

19

Hark! the thrilling symphonies—
Their joyous raptures seize us!
Join we, too, the holy lays,
Jesus, Jesus, Jesus!
Sweetest note in seraph's song.
Sweetest name on mortal tongue,
Sweetest carol ever sung—
Jesus, Jesus, Jesus!

~ Old Hymn.

In the meantime, at Jerusalem, the chief priest and the scribes were plotting how they might destroy him. Many and exciting were the discussions held in the Sanhedrin concerning Jesus. Some few members of the Council, in their inmost hearts, believed he was indeed the Christ, but, through a secret fear of Caiaphas and the chief rulers, they forebore to openly espouse his cause, but quietly used their influence to prevent extreme measures being taken against him. Nicodemus, Gamaliel and Joseph of Arimathea, were especially solicitous that no evil should prevail against him; but, unfortunately, they were decidedly in the minority and could accomplish but little.

After Jesus had healed the impotent man at the Pool of Bethesda, and was assailed by the scribes for healing on the Sabbath day, especially after he had turned upon them with scathing and just rebuke for their hypocrisy,[7] there was a stormy and turbulent session of the Sanhedrin. They sent for Jesus when they had heard of his healing upon the Sabbath day, glad in their hearts of this opportunity to reprove and humiliate him, and he had taken the scourge into his own hands and held them up to the scorn of all who heard him. He had dared to say to them—to them who carried all the wisdom of the age in their wise heads!—"Ye search the Scriptures, because ye think that in them ye have eternal life, and these are they that bear witness of me, and yet ye will not come to me, that ye may have life. I know you, that you have not the love of God in your hearts, else would you receive me, because I come in my Father's name."

It was after Jesus had gone out from their presence that they went into secret session and strove to find some way of compassing his death. They "gnashed upon him with their teeth," and would have sent him to instant death, had the power to do so lain with them. As it did not, they strove to accomplish by strategy what they otherwise could not do. Then it was that Nicodemus, the reticent but the just, said quietly to them, "Must you not first try a man before you condemn him? Is not that the law?" And they had no answer for him, but the taunt, "Wilt thou, too, follow the Nazarene?" Then Gamaliel, looked upon as the wisest man in the council, said:

"Would it not be wise in us to let this matter rest until we see what will become of it? It would be a fearful thing to find that we were fighting against the living God. and this man affirms that he is sent forth by him."

"He is sent forth by the evil one," said Caiaphas, wrathfully. "It is teaching just such doctrines as he teaches that overthrows all civil and religious law."

"I had not heard from reliable sources," said Gamaliel, calmly, "that his teaching was seditious. I have noticed him closely, since, as a boy of twelve, he appeared before us here in the Council; for I was curious to note into what such strange intelligence in one so young would develop."

"Ah!" said Joseph of Arimathea, "I was not a member of the Council at that time, and would be glad to know from one who was present the circumstances as they occurred."

"There was nothing, I think, that you have not probably heard. We were in the midst of a very interesting discussion on some intricate points of the law, when we noticed the boy Jesus in our midst, listening

---

[7] Recorded in St. John. 5th chapter.

with rapt attention to all that was said. No one had seen him enter, or had any idea how he had, unnoticed, gained access to the Council chamber, but his face bore such a look of intense interest, and his deportment was so gentle and at the same time so dignified for one so young, that none were disposed to molest him. Finally he began, with modesty and deference, to ask questions of the members of the Council, some of which we found it difficult to answer; and, if the answer was not perfectly clear and satisfactory to him, it would be followed by questions more searching still, until, in self-defense, as it were, the Council began to question and catechise him. His answers were so clear and so full of wisdom that we were all amazed, and wondered whence he had acquired such knowledge of hidden things. Several hours, full of intense interest to all, had passed, and we were growing more and more astonished at his bearing and his wisdom, when his parents entered, in much agitation, searching for him. It seems that they had left Jerusalem, at the close of the feast, with the caravan that went eastward, in order to return to their home at Nazareth; and, after a day's journey from the city, they discovered that Jesus was not, as they had supposed, with the caravan. Greatly alarmed, they had returned to search for him in the city, and after a vain search for days, at last, in their desperation, they came to the Sanhedrin, where they found him, both listening to the doctors and asking them questions. His mother, overjoyed at finding him, said: 'My son, why didst thou leave us thus? Thy father and I have sought for thee sorrowing.' In reply he turned to his mother respectfully, but with a look upon his face I never could understand, and said: 'Why did ye seek for me? Thou, at least, my mother, shouldest understand that it is time I should begin to look after my Father's business.'"

"There," said Caiaphas, with a sneer, "is where we differ. To my recollection he was arrogant and full of self-conceit. He stole his way into the Council of the most learned men of the nation, and an impertinent child, asked questions that an older and a wiser head would have shrunk from asking. It is that disposition in the boy that has developed and matured him into the pestilent fellow that he has now become. Had we been wise, we would have reproved and punished him then, and nipped in the bud his evil purposes."

"Did he ever return to the Council?" asked Joseph of Arimathea.

"No," answered Gamaliel. "But, curious about the boy, once, sometime afterwards, when passing through Nazareth, I made inquiries concerning him, and found he was living quietly at home with his parents, assisting his father in his work as a carpenter, and was regarded by the community as a remarkably intelligent and dutiful child. His playmates all loved him—called him the 'little prince,' and carried all of their differences to him for arbitration. I called at Joseph's shop, myself, and found Jesus working at his own bench in a remote end of it. Looking up, he at once recognized me. Coming forward and respectfully saluting me, he presented me to his father, and modestly returned to his work. After a few moments' conversation about my journey, Joseph called to Jesus to go into the dwelling and ask his mother to send refreshments for a guest, for the day was warm. The boy obeyed, and during his absence, I questioned concerning him. 'Where had he attended school?' 'Only in the village schools.' 'But this strange knowledge for one so young, as evinced by his questions and answers when before the Council—had he had no skilled instructors in the law?' Joseph was silent for a moment, then said: 'He often bewilders and amazes us by his knowledge, but whence it comes, I know not.' When Jesus returned with the tray, I asked him: 'Will you not again visit the Council chamber?' He hesitated a moment and seemed lost in thought, then turning to me, with the same look upon his face that had attracted my attention when he had addressed his mother that day in this same room, he said, quietly and respectfully: 'Yes, I shall again be there; but not yet for a time.' And with the same courtly bearing I had before observed, he bade me adieu and returned to his work."

Caiaphas had turned many times uneasily in his chair during this conversation, and he now again broke forth wrathfully:

"I tell you, he is a scion of the evil one, and if I had the power, I would have him crucified tomorrow! If he is left to his evil designs, the councils of the Sanhedrin will become a byword and a scorn."

"You may crucify him if you will," said Gamaliel solemnly, "but if he is sowing the seeds of truth, they will live and bear fruit long after he is dead. Truth cannot die. If his works are evil, they will come to naught. Why, then, need we fear him?"

"He *shall* be crucified!" said Caiaphas, rising, his face purple with rage.

"So be it," said Gamaliel, rising with dignity and passing from the room.

20

What means this eager, anxious throng—
Which moves with busy haste along,
These wondrous gatherings day by day—
What means this great commotion, pray?
In accents hushed the throng reply,
"Jesus of Nazareth passeth by."

~ Emma Campbell.

As the days passed, Jesus, watching from the hill upon which Ephraim was situated, saw the caravans of pilgrims beginning to wind down the valley of the Jordan on their approach to Jerusalem for the Feast of the Passover. At length he said to his disciples:

"It is time that we, too, were turning our faces toward Jerusalem."

His disciples had held the secret hope that he might finally abandon what to them seemed so wild a project as going into such imminent peril as his presence in Jerusalem would undoubtedly bring to him. When he had made this quiet assertion, they looked at each other with troubled eyes, but no one ventured to oppose him.

So the little company left the village that had been to them a refuge, and journeyed down into the valley, turning their faces likewise with the crowd toward Jericho.

As they passed through old Jericho, the city of fountains and fragrance and flowers, and as they were entering the new Roman

Jericho, the city of palaces and trees, the multitudes poured forth to meet them, it having become known that the prophet of Nazareth was that day to pass. Just outside the city, upon a little elevation, a few feet only in height, two blind men were sitting, and the hurrying crowd passed them in all directions. They sat silent and listening. A young lad, perhaps eight or nine years old, stood near them, looking eagerly in the direction from which the caravans approached.

"Timothy, laddie," spoke the eldest of the men, "what seest thou now, my son? Has not the prophet yet appeared?"

"No, gran'ther," said the boy; "I see nothing but the caravans approaching, and clouds and clouds of dust."

"He will not look like other men, Timothy," said the old man: "his mien will be stately, and his bearing that of a king."

"He cometh not yet, gran'ther," said the boy, gathering up a handful of pebbles with which he began to play. Presently the old man spoke again:

"Cometh he not yet, laddie?"

And the boy looked again eagerly down the way, then cried out:

"Yes, now he cometh, gran'ther. I see him plainly. He is as you have told me, unlike the other men. He is a king! he surely is a king!"

Then the old man cried aloud:

"Have mercy upon me! Jesus, thou son of David, have mercy upon me!"

And his companion, joining with him, again they cried with shrill voices:

"Have mercy, have mercy upon us, thou son of David!"

The multitude about them, annoyed by their persistent outcry, tried to hush them, and said: "Be silent, fellow's! He will not listen to such as you. Know you not he cometh as a king? Be silent. Hold your peace."

But they cried all the more loudly:

"Have mercy upon us, Jesus, thou son of David!"

And Timothy, eagerly watching Jesus as he approached, cried out:

"Oh, gran'ther! gran'ther! He beckons for thee to come. He surely calls thee to come." And then the people, changing their attitude, said to him:

"Yes, rise, he calleth to thee; take courage and go to him."

And Timothy, leading the two blind men each by the hand, advanced toward Jesus, who had stopped by the wayside, awaiting them. When they had approached him, he said:

"What wouldest thou, Bartimeus, that thou callest thus to me?"

Clasping his hands in entreaty, the old man said:

"Lord, that I may receive my sight."

Jesus looked with compassion upon him, and putting forth his hand, gently touched the closed eyelids, saying to him at the same moment:

"Thy faith hath saved thee. Go in peace." He also touched the lids of the companion of Bartimeus, and the sight returned into his hitherto sightless eyes.

As Bartimeus stood before him with bowed head, when the light came again into his eyes he was looking down, and for the first time, saw the face of the young lad who had so faithfully led him over the rough places in their daily walk. Dropping upon his knees he clasped his arms about him and cried:

"Timothy, laddie, he has given me back my sight. Worship him! Worship him!"

And the young boy, kneeling down, kissed again and again the sandaled feet of Jesus. Then looking up eagerly into his face he cried:

"Thou art a king! Thou art indeed a king!" Jesus laid his hand caressingly upon the dark head of the boy, and said to him gently:

"Timothy,[8] thou hast led the feet of the blind into the smoothest paths by the wayside that thou couldest find. In the days to come, my son, thou wilt lead many from the darkness of sin into the light of God's love. Be thou faithful."

And the boy said earnestly:

"Teacher, I will."

Then, turning to the two men whose sight he had restored, Jesus said:

"Ye have come out of the darkness of your earthly night; walk henceforth in the light that God shall show you."

Then the procession of people, which had stopped and surrounded Jesus when he called the blind men to him, started again toward Jericho, singing and shouting and praising God for his great goodness to men.

And the boy walked close beside Jesus.

---

[8] Not intended to be identified with the friend of Paul.

21

"THE PALMS," BY J. FAURE.
Translated by Ruter William Springer.[9]
All 'round our way palm branches and bright flowers
In rich profusion hang, this festal day:
Jesus draws near, to dry these tears of ours;
Already throngs prepare to welcome pay.
All nations sing with one accord,
With ours your voices blend in adoration,
Hosanna! Praise ye the Lord!
Blessed is he who comes bringing salvation!
He lifts his voice: the people, at the tone,
Their liberty, which they had lost, regain;
Humanity to each his rights doth own,
And light to everyone is given again.
All nations sing, etc.
Rejoice, e'en thou, holy Jerusalem!
Sing freedom now for every child of thine;
By his great love, the God from Bethlehem
Brings them, through faith, the light of hope divine.
All nations sing, etc.

---

[9] As my mother has inserted this without my knowledge, and I do not feel at liberty now to withdraw it. It should be stated that this translation was made, not with the purpose of avoiding previous translations—which have sometimes been quite closely followed—but in order to more accurately express throughout the meaning and spirit of the original.—R. W. S.

It was not Jesus' intention to go at once into the city of Jerusalem nor to remain there after having reached it, so he turned his steps towards Bethany, and went to the house that so often had been to him a home of comfort and pleasure—the house of Lazarus and Mary and Martha. Here he remained for several days preceding Passover Week. But on Sunday morning (the day after the Jewish Sabbath, which we now celebrate as Palm Sunday), he said to his disciples:

"We will go into the city."

They started in the early morning, and he said to John and Peter:

"Go into the village of Bethphage, and in a certain street you will see a donkey with her young colt tied; loose them and bring them hither. If their master should in any way oppose you, simply say to him, 'The Lord hath need of them,' and he will let them go."

They did as he had bidden them, and when they had come to the place, behold, they found it all as Jesus had said, and they took the donkey and brought her, with her foal, to Jesus. And they spread their garments upon the young colt, "upon which never before man had sat," and placed Jesus thereon.

The crowds of caravans proceeding to Jerusalem had now grown very great, and when the people heard that the prophet of Nazareth was also coming, they pressed forward from the village to see him; so the caravans behind and the crowds that came out to meet him, made an immense throng. When they saw Jesus, they hailed him as their king, and the people sang hosannas; they cut down branches from the palm trees that grew by the wayside and spread in his way; the little children lifted up their happy voices and sang aloud, "Hosanna to Jesus, the Son of David, who cometh in the name of the Lord." They gathered the lilies and the wild flowers that grew in abundance by the wayside and spread them before him in the road; they wove garlands and hung them about him; and the air was full of hallelujahs and rejoicings, for the king who was coming in the name of the Lord.

Miriam and Marcus had early gone forth to meet the pilgrims, knowing well that Jesus would be in their midst. When they saw him, they pressed through the crowd until they reached his side. Miriam, looking up into Jesus' face, said:

"Hail, great teacher and beloved king!" Jesus looked down with tenderness into her uplifted eyes, and said:

"Be this a day full of blessings to thee, my daughter?"

She had gathered, as she came along, one great, beautiful, white lily, with its long staff-like stem, and she now held it towards him and said simply:

"My teacher!"

He took it from her hand, and again looking down tenderly upon her, held it as a scepter as he rode onward.

The little children still ran, waving their branches and crying aloud with glad voices:

"Hosanna! Hosanna to Jesus, who cometh as king in the name of the Lord!"

The priests and scribes, who saw the worship that the people offered Jesus, were very angry in their hearts, and planned what they might do to destroy him.

Reaching the point in the hillside road that overlooks Jerusalem, Jesus stopped, with the crowd surrounding him. It was a magnificent view, as all travelers who have seen it must recognize. The great city, lying upon the opposite hill, with its domes and pinnacles and the white and golden Temple breaking in bewildering beauty upon the sight, called forth the admiration of every beholder.

And Jesus, looking down upon it, felt his heart torn within him. He knew, with his prophetic insight, what evil would befall it. He longed to save it from the destruction that he knew awaited it, yet felt he could not, and in the deep anguish of his heart, he cried aloud: "If thou hadst known, even thou, at least in this thy day, the things which belong unto thy peace! But now they are hid from thine eyes. For the days shall come upon thee, that thine enemies shall cast a trench about thee and compass thee round and keep thee in on every side."[10]

---

[10] This terrible prophecy of the destruction of this beautiful city was literally fulfilled thirty-five years later, when Titus with his army bore down and actually destroyed it. The prophecy that "Not one stone should be left standing upon another," was also literally fulfilled. At this day the traveller will find in one or two places the remnants of the massive wall that skirted the great city; and the few broken-hearted Jews who now inhabit a portion of the city assemble on every Friday before these ruins, each dressed in the shroud in which he will sometime be buried, and their voices mingle in pitiful lamentations over the destruction of the city that was once their pride and glory. One who has recently visited the city in its desolation records this scene as one of the most pathetic ever beheld. The priest, surrounded by his handful of followers, breaks forth into the lamentation:

Priest: "For the palace which is destroyed,"

Reaching the foot of Mount Moriah, upon which the Temple stood, the crowd melted slowly away, since processions of pilgrims who were travel-worn and dusty were not permitted. Ascending to the Temple, he entered by the Shushan gate and proceeded at once to the Court of the Gentiles, or outer court of the Temple, the children still accompanying him, shouting their hosannas. Jesus was grieved to see this Court of the Gentiles profaned by venders of merchandise, and the thousands of strangers who had come to Jerusalem buying here their offerings for the sacrifice. Herds of cattle and sheep trod upon and befouled the beautiful, tessellated floor of the court, and made the hot air still more unbearable by their wretched bleating and bellowing. The venders of doves grouped their cages about the massive pillars that formed the long colonnades, and the usurious and greedy money changers placed their tables, covered with coins of different denominations and nationalities

---

People: "We sit down and weep."

Priest: "For the walls which had been thrown down,"

People: "We sit down and weep."

Priest: "For the majesty which has departed,"

People: "We sit down and weep."

Priest: "For the great men who lie dead,"

People: "We sit down and weep."

Priest: "For the precious stones that are burned,"

People: "We sit down and weep."

Priest: "For our priests who have stumbled,"

People: "We sit down and weep."

Priest: "For our kings who have despised him,"

People: "We sit down and weep."

Priest: "We beseech thee, O Lord, have mercy upon us,"

People: "Gather thou the children of Jerusalem."

Priest: "Make haste, O Redeemer of Zion,"

People: "Speak to the heart of Jerusalem."

Priest: "Let beauty and majesty surround Zion."

People: "Turn thy mercy unto Jerusalem."

Priest: "Let the kingdom soon return to Zion,"

People: "And the branch spring forth at Jerusalem."

in the most conspicuous places in the thoroughfare, and all bartered and sold with as much avaricious greed as they would have done in their shops and offices elsewhere. Jesus looked upon the revolting scene with righteous indignation, and the men shrank before his angry glance.

Then they brought to him many who were sick, and he healed them, and he taught the multitude, as they crowded about him, the wonderful doctrine of the New Covenant, and many believed on him because of his gracious words and manner. The children thronged about him, continuing their songs of praise, and chanted with their glad young voices:

"Hosanna! Hosanna! Hosanna to our King!

Oh, earth be glad! Oh, isles rejoice! Oh, courts of heaven ring!

For he cometh in the name of the Lord, For he healeth by the power of his word.

Of David's line, of birth divine!

Oh, earth, receive thy King!

Hosanna! Hosanna! in the highest, sing!

Hosanna! to the Son of David: Priest and King!"

The chief priests and scribes and elders, watching from a distance, chafed and raged and longed to arrest him, but dared not do so, for they feared the people would rise against them.

"He is a sorcerer; he hath bewitched them all!" they cried. And at last, unable longer to keep quiet, and hoping that perchance they might find something in his reply with which to condemn him, they approached him with the question:

"Hearest thou what these say?"

Jesus answered them:

"Have ye never read, 'Out of the mouths of babes thou hast perfected praise'?"—and they could answer nothing.

Two days later, in his terrible denunciation in the Temple, on the last day of his public ministry there, he again broke forth into lamentations, and thus apostrophized Jerusalem:

"Oh, Jerusalem, Jerusalem, thou that killest the prophets and stonest them which are sent unto thee, how often would I have gathered thy children together, even as a hen gathereth her chickens under her wings, and ye would not! Behold, your house is left unto you desolate!"

He had come to Jerusalem her king, and her inhabitants had met him with stoning and abuse. He had come to her to be crowned as her lawful sovereign, and already the gnarled wood had been hewn that should be made into the cross upon which he would be crucified.

On the day after his triumphant entry into Jerusalem, Jesus again entered the Temple court. He looked with still stronger indignation upon the desecration of that sacred place by the sellers and money changers, who had braved his warning glances of the day before. Then he turned upon them and drove them out, men and cattle alike. He bade the venders of doves at once remove their cages, and upset the tables of the money changers, sending their scattered coin rolling in every direction amid the filth of the floor.

"It is written: 'My house shall be called a house of prayer,' but you have made it a den of thieves," he said to them in his indignant majesty.

They remembered how he had previously driven them forth, and now they all fled before him in affright and consternation. After his one invective, he stood in silent dignity and watched the wild scene of confusion and flight. Even the money changers for once forgot their greed of gain and fled, not even stopping to collect their widely scattered coins.

Marcus and Miriam, hurrying forward, had reached the outer court of the temple just as Jesus raised the scourge to drive forth the money changers, and standing apart from the crowd, had witnessed the impressive scene.

"If I had no other proof of his divinity than this," said Marcus, in awe, "I should know him to be divine. Think of a great crowd like that fleeing in terror from one man! And it is the second time it has occurred. Do you not remember, he drove all forth in the same way the first year of his ministry, while yet he was scarcely known as a prophet? Under ordinary circumstances one strong man could have overpowered him, yet with his single arm uplifted against thousands, all fled before him! What but divine power could have produced such a result?"

"Oh, he is the very Christ—the Holy One of God! Who can doubt it?" said Miriam, a great pride and joy swelling her heart and shining in her eyes. "But see, Marcus, the woman trying to save her little child!"

"Oh, I must touch him, Marcus—the blessed Christ!" said Miriam, with clasped hands, as Jesus turned away.

He heard her voice—ever was he quick to hear the voice of love—and stayed, for an instant, his rapid steps to turn his tender eyes upon her and take her outstretched hand within his own.

"Wilt thou not come to us when the day is done, my teacher?" urged Miriam, softly. "Our home is always thine, thou knowest well."

"I know it well, indeed, my daughter, but I must return to Bethany tonight." Then noting the disappointment in her face, he said, "Why cannot thou and Marcus accompany me this night to Bethany? Thou knowest how welcome you both will be at the house of your cousins, Mary and Martha. Will you not go?" Miriam's face brightened with joy.

"May we, oh, may we indeed accompany thee?" Then turning to her husband she said, "Marcus, thinkest thou that we may go?"

"I am sure, my Miriam, that we may go wherever the great teacher will have us."

"Then," said Jesus, "if you will meet me here toward the hour of sunset, we will take that walk together."

So it came to pass that at the sunset hour, Jesus, accompanied by Marcus and Miriam, returned to Bethany, where a warm welcome awaited each of them.

That walk over the sides of Mount Olivet was one that lived forever in the memory of Miriam and Marcus. Jesus, in his heart, had determined that only joy and pleasure should be given them that last hour they were to spend together alone. No reference whatever was made to the trial that lay before him, nor to the trying scenes through which he that day had passed. But he seemed to think of everything beautiful and comforting of which he could speak to them. As they passed along, he pointed out the beautiful scenery that lay beneath them, and though their eyes rested upon the Garden of Gethsemane—which lay at their feet at one point in the road—where he knew that before many another night should pass, his terrible agony must be suffered, yet he only pointed out to them the beauties of the place, and looked across the valley to the shining walls of the temple.

With Miriam, he gathered clusters of flowers, which were growing along the wayside, that they might carry them to Martha for the adornment of her house, and he called the attention of Marcus and Miriam to the beautiful colors and tints of the different plants they gathered.

Then, as the stars began to look forth one by one from the blue heavens above, he spoke of the wonders of the heavenly world, and told of the glories that there lay hidden, unseen by mortal eyes. He dwelt upon the goodness of the Father in so clothing the world that it was full of beauty for his children, and with half a sigh, regretted that they did not better appreciate his love.

Miriam was, by distant ties, related to the two sisters, Mary and Martha, and a warm friendship existed between them; hence she was sure of a welcome, go when she would. To Jesus it was always a second home, where he found the rest and quiet that awaited him nowhere else.

After the evening repast was over, they all ascended to the roof together, and in the silver paschal moonlight, held sweet converse of the years that had passed, and of the days that were to come. Jesus spoke very plainly to them of his approaching departure, and while their hearts were wrung with anguish, they yet were uplifted by the sense of his unmistakable divinity. The little group gathered about him was pathetic. He sat in their midst, with Martha upon his right hand and Marcus and Peter and James surrounding him, while Miriam and Mary, with their arms intertwined, sat at his feet, the golden head resting upon the darker one and the earnest, loving faces upturned to his in adoration. They had talked much of the days that were near at hand, and the tears were slowly trickling over the cheeks of the two young women seated at his feet, when Mary said:

"Why is it necessary that thou shouldest go to Jerusalem at all? Is not the world wide enough, is there not enough for thee to do elsewhere, without exposing thyself to this terrible calamity that awaits thee there?"

"Miriam, my daughter," said Jesus, "canst thou tell aught that I have said to thee as we sat in the starlight on thy father's roof?"

"Yes," said Miriam, the light springing into her dark eyes, "thou didst tell us of the Father's kingdom and of the 'house of many mansions' that stood in the midst of his kingdom. And thou didst tell us that it was necessary that thou shouldest go, in order to prepare a home for each of us there, and that thou wouldest return, at some future time, and take us to share it with thee."

"Yes," said Jesus, "thou art right, my daughter. And what said I of the length of time that must elapse before I should see thee again after having laid down my life?"

"Three days," said Miriam, her fair face growing very white as she still looked upward into the beloved face. "Three days, thou hast said, would elapse before thou shouldest return.[11] But can it be? I cannot but believe every word that thou hast spoken, yet, though I know that in the resurrection thou shalt rise again, I cannot quite grasp the truth that thou wilt come to us again after three days."

"Thou must believe it, Miriam," said Jesus, tenderly, "for therein lies the strength that must sustain thee in the days so near at hand. On this third day comfort will come to thee and will abide; and thou must hold this knowledge fast within thy heart, if thou wouldest be victorious for me over pain and death." So he comforted them during the hours they

---

[11] 'Matt. 20: 19.

sat together, and when at last he left them (for he did not sleep within the little house at Bethany, but went apart with his disciples), in spite of all the agonizing thoughts of the sorrow just in store for them, their hearts were comforted, and more than ever they believed he was the true Messiah for whom they had all watched and waited.

22

Gethsemane! Gethsemane!
My heart in sadness turns to thee.
I hear the moans, the anguished prayer
Borne upward on the still night air;
I feel the dreadful agony
Preceding that on Calvary,
Where Jesus died for you—for me!
Gethsemane! Gethsemane!

~ R. R. S.

The same day that Jesus purified the temple, he taught there openly. The Scribes and Pharisees and all the members of the Sanhedrin, especially enraged by his defiance of them, came to him with perplexing and insulting questions, and strove by every possible means to thwart and trouble him, but on every occasion they were confused and overthrown.

On this last day of his public appearance in the temple, which was on Tuesday of Passover Week, the taunts and threats of the Scribes and even of members of the Sanhedrin that crowded around him to annoy and perplex, seemed to fill the cup of his righteous indignation to overflowing, and he turned upon them with that scathing and terrible denunciation that St. Matthew has recorded.[12] They chafed beneath

---
[12] Matt. 23.

his burning words, and had they dared, they would have sacrificed him that moment, even within the holy walls of the temple; but they feared the people, and they felt that the time was approaching when he could no longer escape them. That very night they held the council that doomed him to an ignominious and almost immediate death. It is not to be wondered at that the Sanhedrin were afraid of the teachings of Jesus. His life must pay the forfeit.[13]

Jesus knew that henceforth the gates of the temple were closed to him, that he had spoken the last words he ever would speak within the walls of his Father's house, and his heart was very heavy within him.

His disciples, strange as it may seem, did not, apparently, understand the situation. They could not realize that he whom they regarded as the real Messiah could suffer the ignominious death of which he told them. For some reason their senses seemed to be blunted, and the consolation they might have given him at times was, for that reason, withheld. To Jesus' human sensibilities, this must have added deeply to his trial, but he looked upon it all with the divine compassion of his nature, and condemned them not.

On Wednesday of that week we have no record of the whereabouts of Jesus; not even the inmates of the house at Bethany caught sight of his beloved face, and his disciples do not seem to have been with him. Doubtless he spent those last hours alone with the Father in some secluded spot. But, when the twilight was falling on Thursday evening, he suddenly appeared to Mary and Martha and held a few moments' comforting converse with them, and between him and Lazarus, so well beloved, there was an interview, the memory of which remained with Lazarus during all the remaining years of his life. Then, with his disciples, he started for his last walk over the pleasant road that led across Olivet to Jerusalem. He saw Gethsemane at his feet, and also dimly saw Calvary lying across the valley. But no word of lamentation broke from him now. Silently, and with a certain kingly dignity that he never seemed to have worn before with all of his divinity, he passed on, and his disciples, recognizing the sublimity of his mien, walked a little distance behind him. The silent majesty of his demeanor seemed to forbid familiar intercourse, and so they talked in whispers and left him to the solitude of his own thoughts upon this journey.

---

[13] Their chief motive (John 11:48) was a fear that Jesus would start another unsuccessful insurrection, and thus bring them further disaster. They understood neither his motives, methods nor power. —R.W.S.

It seems strange that no record is made of his having been met by any of his enemies or friends on this last evening, but the city was approached in silence, and by a quiet street, they reached the house wherein the upper chamber lay where their last supper would be celebrated.

After reaching Jerusalem they went in a group directly to the quiet house at the head of the narrow street. They were silently admitted by Marcus, and proceeded directly to the upper room.

Jesus was the last to enter. The "goodman of the house" had excluded his servants from the front entrance, that a greater privacy might be secured for Jesus. Marcus stood just within the gate, that no intrusions might occur, and his father stood at the foot of the outside stairway that led to the upper room, so as to make it impossible for any to enter there without his knowledge.

In talking with Marcus some hours before, his father said:

"There is something in the air that I do not like and cannot understand. All day long a strange hush seems to have fallen upon the city. Men stand apart in groups and talk, yet more than once, when I have approached them, they have suddenly separated and gone their ways, as though they were talking of that which they would not have me hear. If I knew the meaning of fear, I would say it had taken strange possession of my heart. I wish the night were past and the morning here."

And Marcus had answered him:

"I understand thee well, my father. That same mysterious dread has compassed me the entire day. There is something evil brooding in the air. Miriam feels it as much as we. She tossed upon her bed and moaned in her restless sleep last night, or started up, crying, 'Marcus, they have taken him!' And what can I say to comfort her? Only this: we know, my father, the power is within him to avert all evil, and if he permits it, there is surely a reason beyond our comprehension why it should be. This is my only comfort."

His father sighed heavily, as he said:

"Yes, it is our only hope, but, since he is divine, why may he not thwart the plans of these evil men, and at least save himself from a cruel death?"

When Jesus entered the house and saw Marcus standing alone within the entrance, he paused an instant, and taking the hands of the young man within his own, he looked down into the depths of the uplifted eyes and said, with visible emotion:

"John Mark, be thou faithful to the end, and thy reward awaits thee. God fill thy heart with peace."

Then, bending over, he kissed him on both cheeks, and turning, approached the stairway. Here he confronted the man so long and secretly his friend. He placed a hand upon either shoulder, and looking into his eyes with the same earnest look with which he had regarded Marcus, he whispered:

"Faithful and true! Faithful and true! David, beloved friend, thy room in my Father's house of many mansions is ready and will await thy coming. I shall soon greet thee there."

Then he embraced him, and turning, he went to the ever-hallowed "upper room" and closed the door behind him.

How our hearts thrill, after all these ages, at the mention of that sacred "upper room"! How we long to know what passed behind the closed doors, after Jesus and his disciples had entered therein! But mystery and sorrowful surmisings surround it. Only through the Evangelists are we certain of a few of the events that transpired there that night.

We know that Judas, the traitor, crept from the room with a curse upon his life. We know, too, that at the close of that memorable supper, the last that Jesus was ever to eat with his disciples upon earth, he took bread, blessed and break it, and passed it to each of them in turn, saying:

"Eat; this is my body that was broken for you."

And that, likewise, he took the cup and gave it to his disciples, saying:

"Drink all ye of this; it is my blood of the new testament, which is shed for you and for many, for the removal of sins."

Thus was instituted the blessed sacrament, which, down to this time, is still held in such reverence by all who are his disciples.

We know, too, that on that blessed night he gave to them, and through them unto us, the new commandment, "Love ye one another, even as I have loved you." Not with the ordinary love men bear to one another, but with the deep, divine love that he, as their teacher, bore for them. It was the New Covenant that has come down to us, changing our lives from human to divine.

"Even as I have loved you, love ye one another."

Ah! if we kept this command to its fulfillment, what a changed world this would be in which we live!

The evening so eventful to this little band of his disciples was drawing to a close, and Jesus, arising from his seat at the table, said:

"We will sing a hymn before we part."

We may imagine that, among others, they then together sang the beautiful Psalm of David:

"The Lord is my shepherd; I shall not want.

"He maketh me to lie down in green pastures: he leadeth me beside the still waters.

"He restoreth my soul: he leadeth me in the paths of righteousness for his name's sake.

"Yea, though I walk through the valley of the shadow of death, I will fear no evil: for thou art with me; thy rod and thy staff, they comfort me.

"Thou preparest a table before me in the presence of mine enemies; thou anointest my head with oil; my cup runneth over.

"Surely goodness and mercy shall follow me all the days of my life: and I will dwell in the house of the Lord forever."

And Jesus knew, though his disciples did not fully realize it, that it was through this "valley of the shadow" that he was now to walk but he was equally sure that the great Shepherd would be with him and make even his agonized journey to lie through green valleys and beside still waters.

Then they went forth quietly, Peter and James and John keeping especially near the Master. Down through the quiet streets they passed, for the hour was now growing late, and a strange hush seemed to rest upon the entire city. Crossing the brook Kedron, they went into the Garden of Gethsemane. It was there that they had often spent the nights together in holy converse, or in restful sleep, but now a strange awe seemed to hold the disciples, so that they had no questions to ask and no remarks to make to their beloved teacher. He seemed, this night, apart from them; a veil had fallen between their faces and his, which they could not penetrate. When they paused beneath one of the great olive trees for which the garden was noted, Jesus said:

"Sit ye here while I go yonder and pray." He went apart into a secluded place, taking with him only Peter and James and John. Here he said to them:

"My soul is exceeding sorrowful, even unto death; abide ye here and watch, while I go a little further."

Jesus went about a stone's throw beyond them and knelt down and prayed, "Father, all things are possible to thee: if thou be willing, let this affliction pass from me. Still, not what I wish, but what thou hast planned." Then there appeared to him an angel from heaven, strengthening him. Jesus, being in still greater agony, prayed even more earnestly, and his sweat became as it were great drops of blood, falling down upon the ground.

Presently he arose from prayer and came back to the three disciples, and found them sleeping. Jesus said to Peter: "Simon! thou asleep!

Couldest thou not watch with me, even one hour? Rouse thee and pray, that thou mayest not again yield to temptation; thou art willing enough, but tired in body."

Again Jesus went away and prayed, "Oh, my Father! if I must undergo this, thy will be done."

Once more Jesus returned and again found the three sleeping, for their eyes were heavy. When he awoke them, they could give him no excuse for their neglect.

Then Jesus left them the third time and prayed again, as he had prayed the second time.

The third time he returned to the three disciples and said to them, "Are you sleeping on, then, and taking your rest? The time is past; the hour is come when the Son of man is to be betrayed into the hands of sinners. Arise, let us be going. See! the betrayer is coming!"

He turned and struggled with his captor.

In the meantime the house in the narrow street, in which the upper room lay, was quite deserted. The lights were put out, the doors were fastened, and the inmates, worn out with the heat and anxieties of the day, had laid them down for a brief repose. Miriam tossed restlessly upon her couch, her mind filled with strange and terrible forebodings. The night was warm and sultry, even for that time and climate, and Marcus had removed his undergarment and lain down with only the linen sheet about him. Like Miriam, he, too, was very restless, and sleep refused to close his eyes. Suddenly, an indistinct murmur aroused him from partial insensibility, and at the same instant, Miriam, wrapped only in a loose night robe, rushed into his room, crying:

"Marcus! Marcus! The house is surrounded by a crowd of evil men, and they are clamoring for thee to open the door! What can they seek? Not Jesus, oh, not Jesus!"

Marcus gathered the linen sheet about him, and—with a passing word of comfort and courage to Miriam, he ran to the window, to see, indeed, a crowd of men, many of whom in the moonlight he recognized as the most violent opposers of Jesus, turning away from the house, as they seemed to be convinced the object of their search was not within.

"Oh!" said Marcus, "they are seeking Jesus to destroy him! I must give him warning." And Miriam cried out:

"Wait not for anything! Go at once!" Marcus hastily slipped his feet into his sandals, and forgetting to put on his inner garment, whispered hurriedly to Miriam:

"Be strong, be strong, my wife; I will follow them stealthily until I see where they are going. If I find they are really seeking Jesus, I will manage to elude them and reach him first, so as to give him warning of their approach." Keeping closely in the shadows of the houses, he followed the crowd cautiously, until he saw that their steps were bending toward Gethsemane. Then, by a quieter but somewhat longer route, he hastened thither, always well concealed, that none might intercept him on the way. He reached the garden too late; the crowd was returning, with Jesus bound in their midst. Marcus slipped nimbly among them, and catching Jesus eagerly by the arm, he cried to him in an earnest whisper:

"Oh, flee, my Master, while there is yet time! Use thy divine power! I implore thee! I implore thee, flee while there is yet time!" But Jesus, looking upon him with compassion, whispered in return:

"It must be thus; the hour indeed has come. Leave me, for the sake of Miriam and the work for me thou hast to do."

Marcus was by this time observed. One rude fellow caught him by his garment to detain him, crying:

"This fellow is one of them, for I have often seen him with Jesus."

Jesus again said to Marcus, "Go!"

Knowing that, alas! he could be of no benefit to the teacher he so loved, he turned, struggled with his captor, and finally, leaving his clothing in the hands of the man who had sought to detain him, he escaped, hid amid the dense shadows of the trees, and then, brokenhearted, crept back the way he had come to his father's house.[14]

---

[14] The above hypothetical reconstruction of the adventure of this "Young man with a linen sheet" (Mark 14:51-52), taken together with the fact that St. Mark is the only chronicler of the event, offers quite strong proof that he was himself the hero of the adventure.— R. W. S.

23

There is a green hill far away
Without the city wall,
Where the dear Lord was crucified,
Who died to save us all.
There was no other good enough
To pay the price of sin:
He only could unlock the gate
Of heaven, and let us in.

~ C. F. ALEXANDER.

The events of Jesus' arrest, betrayal and trial have been too vividly recorded by the Evangelist to require repetition. From the court of the Sanhedrin to the palace of Pilate, we all know how he was hurried. We know that, but for Pilate's weakness, he would have been acquitted, for Pilate said to the multitude, "I find no fault in this man."

Of the insult, the outrage, the cruelty, inflicted that day upon our Lord, we forbear to speak, for, through the centuries down to the present hour, the memory of them brings the hot blood of indignation to the heart and the tear of anguished sorrow to the eyes. Second only to his love for his followers is the love they carry for him, from generation to generation, within their hearts.

After the insult and ignominy of his mock trials, the boisterous procession started on its way to Calvary.

He who had come to Jerusalem a king, now bore upon his shoulders the cross hewn from the gnarled wood, and staggered along the dusty road beneath its weight.

The day was oppressively hot and the roads were dusty and unclean, as were always the narrow streets of this great city. The crowd surged and thronged about him, but, even in his agony, he was silent and godlike, as he struggled on beneath the weight of the heavy cross.

Miriam and Marcus had started out early, for Miriam had said to her husband, "Do not deny me the privilege of being near him in these last hours." And Marcus had reluctantly consented.

Now, through the dusty streets, she managed to keep but a little distance from Jesus in his toilsome ascent to Calvary.

The road became steeper and more stony, and the weight of the cross more and more insupportable. At length the human strength of Jesus yielded, and he sank, fainting, beneath its weight. His fall caused a short stop in the forward movement of the procession. Miriam, seizing her opportunity, darted forward, and reaching the side of Jesus, she drew her kerchief from her bosom, and bending over, wiped the perspiration from his white face.[15]

His falling had created a commotion among the guard. They saw he could not reach the place of crucifixion beneath his grievous burden, and seizing hold of a young countryman who was walking near, they laid the cross upon his shoulders, and he bore it to the end.

The summit of the little hill was reached; the three holes in which the three crosses were to be placed had already been dug. The soldiers ordered back the crowd and formed a circle about the prisoners, and each man was stretched upon his cross ready for execution.

When Miriam saw her beloved teacher stretched thus upon his cross, her already white face showed such deathly pallor and she leaned so heavily upon her husband that he feared her strength would entirely desert her. He drew her gently as far from the circle as she would permit him to do, and supporting her with his left arm, he pressed her head against his breast and covered her ear with his palm, to deaden, if possible, the sounds of the hammer, as the cruel nails entered the flesh.

The two thieves, amid piercing shrieks and groans, were first fastened to their separate crosses, and these were then set up in their respective places. Then came the terrible ordeal, when Jesus, too, must suffer.

It was then that Marcus, looking with strained eyes upon the beloved Christ, as they stretched his prostrate form upon the cross, saw the pallid lips part and heard the faint prayer:

---

[15] Tradition ascribes this act to a woman named Veronica, and asserts that the image of Jesus's face was miraculously fixed on the cloth. —R. W. S.

"Father, forgive them; for they know not what they do."

Was ever love or forgiveness such as this!

At the first stroke of the dreaded hammer, Miriam trembled and shrank, until her husband feared even for her reason. She struggled bravely, her face like death itself, the dark circles beneath her eyes extending even down upon her pallid cheeks, and when she heard no moan, no cry from the white lips of Jesus, she felt she must be brave, and for his sake, bear silently this anguish.

Near the cross, after it was erected, stood a few women with pallid faces and broken hearts. Among them, Jesus recognized the beloved face that had smiled upon him first in his divine childhood. He saw upon her face the agony from which he would fain have saved her, if he might. He looked down upon her with love in his dying eyes and whispered:

"Mother, John will be thy son."

Turning his gaze upon his beloved disciple, he said:

"Behold thy mother."

And the tender arm of John immediately supported her, and from that hour, he took the place assigned him by his dying Master.

A dark pall seemed to envelop the sun.

About noon a dark pall seemed to envelope the sun, and an inky blackness settled down over all the land; the air grew cold and clammy, and above all, a terrible hush and a sense of foreboding came upon the people. More and more oppressive became the awful sense of horror. The nerves were strained to the utmost, as if preparing for some terrible crash. About three o'clock Aurelius, of the household of Caiaphas, mounted upon his horse, rode up as near the foot of the cross as the guard would permit him to come. He held in his hand an uplifted spear, with which he strove to smite the dying Christ, and tauntingly he cried:

"Thou who savest others, save now thyself; come down from the cross and show to us thou art divine."

Only his form could dimly be seen in the darkness, but his rasping voice smote all ears with a tone of demoniac triumph.

Marcus thought: "Hell is rejoicing." And then, "Will Jesus answer this taunt? What triumphant message will he fling back?"

There was a moment's awful hush. Then from the cross, in tones low, pleading, indescribably pathetic, came the words, "My God! my God! Why hast thou forsaken me?"

Would God reply? Jesus had referred Aurelius' taunt to Him who had said, "Judgment is mine; I will repay." The suspense at last became unbearable, and Marcus whispered, half aloud, "God must answer, or there is no God!"

"Hush!" said Miriam, "it is the Psalm, 'The Hind of the Morning.' It goes on to say:[16] He hath not despised nor abhorred the affliction of the afflicted; neither hath he hid his face from him; but when he cried unto him, he heard.'"

Again they were waiting to see what would happen. The Roman soldiers, mistaking the Hebrew words, thought Jesus had called for Elijah.

Presently, through death-parching lips, "I thirst."

What pity moved the Roman soldier to run to the wine jar, wet a sponge with the sour wine, and putting this on the end of a stick, hold it to the Savior's lips? Even then the others cried out, "Don't! Wait and see if Elijah comes to help him."

The Savior drank. The soldier stood back with the sponge-rod in his hand. The others were still in the same attitude as when they spoke. Aurelius seemed frozen in his attitude of defiance. All could now be plainly seen, for a strange light hung over the cross of Jesus and seemed

---

[16] PS. 22: 24.

to shine from all about him, throwing dark shadows from the other two crosses and from the groups of waiting people.

Suddenly Jesus raised his head. His eyes were gazing out into the other world. He drew himself up, as for a mighty effort, and uttered a shout of triumph: "Finished!"

Then, with the same breath, those who were near heard him say, his gaze still upward:

"Father, into thy hands I commit my spirit."

A convulsive shudder. Then his head sank upon his breast, the limbs relaxed, the light about the cross quickly faded away, until all was the most intense blackness. The Son of God was dead!

Crash! The earth is rocking and cracking. A thunderbolt falls, striking the distant temple and rending in two the curtain before the Holy of Holies. Great crevices open in the earth. Graves are torn open and dead bodies from them are scattered all about.

The horse of Aurelius, rearing and plunging with affright, fell headlong into one of these chasms, and Marcus and Miriam, who saw through the gloom the upturned purple face of the man lying with broken neck beneath the weight of his dead charger, remembered it was he who had reviled and desecrated the dying Son of God, and in their hearts they felt that upon one, at least, of his revilers sure and swift vengeance had come.

The people fell upon their faces, or fled in terror and affright down the mountain into the city, and soon only the Roman guard, with a few of those who loved Jesus best, were left in the midst of the terrible scene. Miriam hid her face in the bosom of her husband, as they still knelt before the cross.

The work of redemption was indeed "finished." Life and light and love had triumphed over sin and darkness and death.

Oh, what a life, what a death, was his! When his executioners drove through the quivering flesh the cruel nails that fastened him to the cross, he only prayed, "Father, forgive them, for they know not what they do." And when, in the midst of his terrible agony and suffering, the voice of the penitent thief fell on his ear, his compassionate heart, still alive to the grief of others, responded to the cry and spoke peace and pardon to the wretched soul.

Marcus and Miriam remained long in meditative silence. The darkness about them gradually lifted a little, and they could see the three dark crosses and hear the groans of the dying thieves. But the figure upon the central cross was still in death. After quite a while a squad of soldiers came up, were admitted by the guard, and immediately fell upon one of the crucified thieves and beat him to death with clubs. Then they went to the other, who had been shrieking for mercy, and served him in like manner. When they came to the body of Jesus, Miriam again hid her face on her husband's breast and sobbed aloud. But the soldiers seemed in doubt. One of them said, "Nothing to do here; he is dead already."

"Impossible!" said another. One who was mounted and seemed to be in command of this party, thrust his spear into Jesus' side. All waited to observe the result; then the spearman said, "He is dead; come away!" And they departed.

Miriam had sunk to the earth, and Marcus knelt beside her, holding her head against his breast. A long time they waited thus, while many others silently withdrew.

At last Marcus, bending low over Miriam, whispered, "Dearest wife, the agony is over; he is at rest. Come with me, beloved; before the day is done let us return. He is not here; we can no longer comfort him."

With a last lingering look at the face of her beloved teacher, Miriam permitted herself to be led away by her husband to their home. For greater privacy, they passed around the city to the westward, intending to enter by a gate near their own home. As they turned southward, they looked back to the place where they had left him. The gloom was lifting, and the dark clouds were now turning to billowy masses of purple and gold. Against these, in distinct outline, arose the figures of the three crosses, illumined by a burst of sunlight from the late afternoon sun. Above them, spanning the entire summit of Calvary, thrown upon the still dark clouds behind was a rainbow—the most beautiful they had ever seen. For some moments they stood in rapt contemplation, while God was speaking to their hearts. Then Miriam, with clasped hands and a look almost of inspiration, said to her husband:

"Oh, Marcus! It is the 'bow of promise'!

It is a sign for us—for us alone. He is the Son of God! More than ever, now I know he is the Son of God. In spite of the deep anguish and sorrow of this crushing hour, there stirs within my heart an almost divine joy, which tells me that, somehow, he is the Son of God."

And Marcus said:

"Yes, dear wife, he is, somehow, the Son of God."

Upon a cross my Savior died,
Behold his wounded hands and side!
He died for you, he died for me,

In that dark hour, on Calvary,
Upon a cross.
Upon a cross, he bowed his head,
Pierced by the cruel thorns, and said:
"Forgive—they know not what they do!" This prayer he made for me, for you,
Upon a cross.
Upon a cross, his life he gave,
A lost and ruined world to save.
Think, when you at its feet bow down,
He won his kingdom and his crown Upon a cross.

24

*Lift your glad voices in triumph on high,
For Jesus hath risen and man shall not die.
Vain were the terrors that gathered around him,
And short the dominion of death and the grave;
He burst from the fetters of darkness that bound him,
Resplendent in glory to love and to save.
Loud was the chorus of angels on high,
The Savior hath risen and man shall not die.*

~ Henry Ware, Jr.

Neither Marcus nor Miriam could ever remember anything about that Sabbath Saturday, the day after the crucifixion. They were in a kind of mental stupor all day. After the excitement and actual sight of the occurrences of that terrible crucifixion day were past, only the awful fact seemed to remain, too appalling to leave room for any other thought: Jesus, their friend, their hoped-for Messiah, was dead—dead and buried. And all his promises and their hope sand even their very lives seemed buried with him in that rocky tomb of which someone had told them, they knew not and cared not who. Oh, yes, it was the faithful Ayeah. But no matter—he was gone! And Miriam remembered, too, afterwards. how, on that terrible Sabbath, she had noticed her bird stirring briskly in its cage, and how she had vaguely wondered why it was not dead.

Her father seemed to be holding some strange kind of reception; for, all day long, the disciples of Jesus kept dropping in, in little groups, wandering through the court and to that "upper chamber," which was henceforth to be their rallying point, and passing out again. They asked for no one and appeared hardly to see anyone, but conversed apart, if at all. And to Miriam and to all that household they seemed only as weird specters from some visionary shore. Only one thing seemed actual and real: the fact that he was dead.

They heard vague rumors, too, that some who had tried to visit the tomb in which his loved remains had hastily been laid, had encountered a body of Roman soldiers guarding the place, who had rudely repulsed them. Thus their spirits sank still lower. A terrible weakness came upon them, with nausea, trembling and inability to stand, until they lay scattered about the house, some on couches or benches, and some even on the bare floors, wherever they could wearily find an asylum. Thus passed the second night, without either sleep or wakefulness, in a stunned stupor.

Sunday morning, the third day, the day after the Sabbath, a little party of disciples, with the members of the household, again found themselves in the upper chamber together. Their number had been diminished by the departure of some from Jerusalem to their homes, and as it was still early, there were many who had not yet come.

Suddenly there came the light sound outside of a woman running, an astonished exclamation from some of those without, the door was burst open, and there entered Mary Magdalene. No pictures could be more in contrast than they and she. The whole room seemed illuminated and vitalized by her presence.

For an instant she clasped her hands and drew herself together, as if to gather additional strength for the explosion that followed, and then burst forth:

"I have seen him! He is risen! He is risen! It is he himself, the Christ! Oh, he is alive! I touched him! He spoke to me! It is really he!" And she danced about the room, weeping and laughing, shaking some of her dearer friends by their shoulders or hands and repeating her message in various forms.

Miriam caught her as she passed and said, "What do you say? Tell us all about the matter."

The others gathered around, and controlling herself, Mary Magdalene said:

"Why, last night I couldn't sleep. Everything seemed so close, I felt I just must get out of doors. When outside, I felt if I could just get a glimpse of the tomb where I had seen his body laid. I could lie down there and be calm. The full moon was nearly down in the west as I came in sight of the place.

"I looked for the Roman guard, but they were nowhere in sight. The tomb was open. I ran quickly and looked in. It was empty!

"I felt sure that his body had been removed elsewhere, and suspected that it had been done by his enemies, who had placed the guard, so I ran and told Peter and John, who were rooming nearby. They ran back ahead of me and then went into the city—I suppose to investigate the matter. I felt so overcome by this new trouble that I remained at the tomb, weeping. I didn't know anybody was inside, but presently I stooped down and looked in, and there I saw two men. I think one of them asked why I was weeping; he spoke very kindly, but I didn't want to talk, so! turned away and nearly ran into another man outside. I thought he was the gardener, but he was the Christ! He spoke to me and asked me why I was weeping. I don't know what I said, for suddenly I saw it was he, and fell at his feet, holding on to him as though he might get away. They were his feet, for there were the prints of the nails. Oh, how I kissed them and held them! At last he said, 'Don't hold on to me so. but go and say to my brethren, I am going up to my Father and your Father, and my God and your God;' so I came to tell you."

Just as she finished, several other women rushed into the room and told the astonished disciples that they, too, had seen the angels in the tomb, and that Jesus himself had met them on their way back. They continued to protest that this was so, but the news seemed so incredible that the disciples could not believe it. They were almost as much stunned by this news as they previously had been by their grief, and knew not what to think.

Marcus and Miriam passed from the room, and Miriam said to him, "I must go to the place, to see for myself." Marcus went with her, but, as they neared the spot, she ran on ahead, her heart full of strange tumult. Would Jesus, the crucified, he who had done so much for her, indeed arise, as he had promised his disciples? Her heartbeat wildly at the thought.

She believed that all Jesus had said must come to pass, and yet there was a secret fear that possibly she had not rightly understood his meaning. Just before reaching the sepulcher, she paused in the midst of her contemplation, and looked with surprise and admiration on the scene before her. The entire ground in the vicinity of the sepulcher was covered with a carpet of blooming flowers.[17] Look where she would, lilies were blooming everywhere. It seemed incredible that they should so soon have sprung and blossomed; her heart gave a great thrill of joy—it was in honor of her coming king!

---

[17] Even to this day the white lilies cover the ground near the sepulcher in profusion.

Marcus and Miriam

A few steps more brought her in sight of the door of the tomb. The great stone was rolled away! Running to the open door, she could plainly see that the body of Jesus no longer lay where it had been placed on the evening of his crucifixion. Before she could question her heart farther, she saw two angels seated, one at the head and one at the foot of the place where he had lain. One of them spoke to her, asking:

"Whom seekest thou? If it is Jesus of Nazareth thou wouldest find, he is not here, for he has risen, as he himself foretold. Go and tell his disciples that their Lord indeed has risen."

Miriam ran back to find her husband, and throwing herself into his arms with a cry of almost hysterical joy, she said:

"Oh, Marcus, he is not here! He has risen, as he has said!"

And he, almost as much excited as herself, cried:

"What is this thou sayest to me, my Miriam? Can it be true that Jesus indeed has risen?"

"Come thou and see," said Miriam, taking his hand and starting eagerly to run back to the sepulcher.

Go and tell his disciples that their Lord indeed has risen.

Reaching it, Marcus bent down, as John had' done, for he could not enter the sacred precincts with sandaled feet. The angels were not there, but when he saw that the tomb indeed was vacant and saw the linen cloths neatly folded and lying by themselves apart, he sank upon the ground, completely overcome by his emotion. Burying his face in his hands, he let his heart arise in silent adoration and praise to his now risen Lord.

Oh, what a day was that in all the homes of these humble men and women! Again and again the happy lips of Miriam broke forth into songs of praise, and again and again she said:

"Oh, Marcus, I knew he was divine!"

And Jairus and his wife, and the father and mother of Marcus, all joined in the general rejoicing, and it seemed that never so bright a day had broken over the city of Jerusalem.

That same evening, as two of the disciples, Cleopas and Andrew,[18] were on their way to Emmaus, a village about seven and a half miles from Jerusalem, they were conversing excitedly of the things that had been told. They had not gone to the tomb, and though they had heard the wonderful tidings of how Jesus had risen, they only knew it from hearsay; and, like Thomas, it was difficult for them to accept the truth, unless their eyes could also bear testimony to it. They wanted to believe, but oftentimes faith is weak, even with those who seek it most.

As they walked onward, a stranger joined himself to them and said:

"Of what do you converse so eagerly?" Cleopas, with a look of surprise, answered: "Art thou a stranger in Jerusalem, that thou dost not know what things have happened there within these last days?"

And the stranger answered them:

"Of what things speak ye?"

Then they told him that all their hopes that Jesus was the Messiah, who was to redeem their people, were lost; they described his terrible agony upon the cross, and how with his death all hope seemed to have vanished from their lives. Their Messiah, their King, had after all proved to be a mortal man. They also told him that certain women had that morning come to the disciples in the upper room, and had told them that on visiting the tomb they found it empty; how they had seen two angels sitting within the tomb and guarding it, who told them that Christ had risen. But this seemed all too incredible for them to believe, and their hearts were still full of sorrow.

---

[18] Possibly.

Then he reproached them for their dullness and their want of faith. "Do you not remember," he asked them, "where Isaiah has written, 'For unto us a child is born, unto us a son is given and the government shall be upon his shoulder; and his name shall be called Wonderful, Counselor. The Mighty God, The Everlasting Father, The Prince of Peace? Of whom, think you, is this written?"

"Of the Messiah, truly," they answered him. "And therefore are our hearts sorrowful, for we had so hoped that Jesus was he of whom the prophet wrote."

"Aye," continued the stranger, "and does not the same prophet say farther on in his prophecy, that he 'shall open the eyes of the blind, and bring the prisoners from the prison, and those that sit in darkness out of the prison-house'?"

"All that Jesus did," said Andrew, "and yet they crucified him."

He answered, "Isaiah also says, 'And the Spirit of the Lord shall rest upon him, the spirit of wisdom and understanding, the spirit of counsel and might, the spirit of knowledge and of the fear of the Lord, and shall make him quick of understanding in the fear of the Lord. With righteousness shall he judge the poor, and reprove with equity for the meek of the earth; and righteousness shall be the girdle of his loins, and faithfulness the girdle of his reins.'"

"Surely that was written of our great teacher," said Cleopas.

Jesus drew from beneath the folds of his tunic the book of the prophet Isaiah, and opening at the fifty-third chapter, read it aloud to the two men as they walked: "He shall grow up before him as a weak plant, and as a root out of dry ground." He dwelt especially upon the passages: "He is despised and rejected of men; a man of sorrows and acquainted with grief. He was oppressed and he was afflicted, yet he opened not his mouth; he is brought as a lamb to the slaughter, and as a sheep before her shearers is dumb, so he opened not his mouth. He was taken from prison and from judgment: and who shall declare his generation? for he was cut off out of the land of the living: for the transgression of my people was he stricken. He made his grave with the wicked and with the rich in his death."

"That prophecy is surely written of Jesus whom they have crucified!" cried the two disciples. "It hath literally been fulfilled in him."

Then, beginning with Moses and the prophets, he expounded unto them all the things that had been prophesied concerning the Messiah, and showed to them how everything had been fulfilled, even to his death and burial. And they were overwhelmed with astonishment, and wondered that they had failed to recognize these truths in themselves.

"Oh, that we had more truly received and known him as the Messiah!" they moaned in their inmost hearts.

When they reached Emmaus, the stranger would have passed onward, but they constrained him to remain, saying to him:

"Abide with us, for the eventide draweth near."

And he went with them into the house, and sat down to their simple repast with them. And he took bread, and blessed, and break it; and instantly their eyes were opened, and they knew it was the Lord who was their guest. But before they could speak or worship him, he had disappeared from their sight. Then how they blamed themselves for their stupidity, and said, one to another:

"Did not our hearts burn within us while he was speaking with us on the way, and while he opened to us the Scriptures?"

And, rising hastily, they returned to Jerusalem and went immediately into the upper room, where the other disciples were gathered; and they told them the rapturous news—how Jesus had risen and had appeared to them on the way—oh, blessed way—to Emmaus! And the disciples greeted them with the same ardent greetings and said:

"He hath appeared also to Simon."

And their hearts were filled with rejoicing and with praise, so that they scarcely knew how to contain themselves. Even while they talked, Jesus himself appeared in their midst, greeting them with the words, "Peace be unto you!" But so sudden was his appearance and so etherealized his person, that they were almost frightened, half believing that it was a spirit that had thus appeared to them. But Jesus said:

"Why are ye troubled, and why do anxious doubts arise in your hearts? Look at my hands and my feet, and see that it is I; handle me and see that I have real flesh and bones, the same as you."

And he showed them his hands and his side, and then, lest they should farther doubt, he Said:

"Have you anything here to eat?"

And they brought him some bread and a piece of broiled fish, and he ate it before them, convincing them thus that he still had human instincts and tastes.

From the moment that Jesus had entered the room, Miriam had stood with her eyes steadfastly fixed upon him, and her hands, closely clasped, pressed tightly against her bosom. After Jesus had eaten, he turned and looked upon her, and going close beside her, Said:

"Miriam, my daughter, said I not truly that I would return to you? It is the third day since they crucified me, and I am here. Dost thou now, my child, believe all I have said to thee about our future life in the 'house of many mansions'?"

And Miriam, looking up earnestly into his eyes, with a look full of love and devotion, reached forth her hand and touched him, as with joy she cried:

"My teacher! Oh, my teacher! I believe! I do believe!"

EASTER HYMN

He is risen! He is risen!
Let the bells of heaven ring.
Crucified, despised, forsaken,
Now we crown him Lord and King.
Let the islands of the sea
Swift repeat the thrilling strain,
Earth reecho joyfully,
Jesus died, but lives again!
Heart of mine, crush back thy pain—
Jesus died, but lives again!
He is risen! He is risen!
From the bonds of death set free,
He ascended unto heaven
There to reign eternally.
Tell, oh tell the wondrous story,
"Christ the Lamb, for sinners slain"—
Myriad saints call back from glory—
"Conquered death and rose again."
Listen to the glad refrain:
"Jesus died, but rose again!"
All the heavenly hosts adore him!
Seraphim and angels sing,
Bending down with joy before him,
"Jesus Christ our Priest and King."
In the ages still before us
All the earth shall own his reign,
Joining. in the angel chorus:
"Jesus died, but rose again.
Though he in the grave hath lain,
Still he rose and lives again!"

THE END.